#3 Stupid Cupids

Look for these and other books
in the Bad News Ballet series:

Bad News Ballet

#3 Stupid Cupids

Jahnna N. Malcolm

AN
APPLE
PAPERBACK

SCHOLASTIC INC.
New York Toronto London Auckland Sydney

ISBN 0-590-42474-2

12 11 10 9 8 7 6 5 4 3 2 1   9/8 0 1 2 3 4/9

Printed in the U.S.A.   11

First Scholastic printing, June 1989

*FOR MARIE MATHAY
MY VERY BEST FRIEND
IN THE WHOLE WIDE WORLD.*

Chapter One

"It's a boy!" Gwendolyn Hays shouted as she raced into the dressing room of the Deerfield Academy of Dance.

"Congratulations!" Rocky Garcia tugged her wild dark hair into a ponytail and added, "I think."

Zan Reed, a thin black girl, looked up from the book she was reading and exclaimed, "Oh, that's truly wonderful!"

"I didn't even know your mother was pregnant," Mary Bubnik drawled. "She looked so thin and all."

Gwen dropped her canvas dance bag down on the bench and put her hands on her hips. "What are you guys talking about?"

"Your new baby brother," Mary Bubnik replied.

1

Gwen rolled her eyes. "I don't have a baby brother. I'm talking about the boy in the front office."

"So?" Rocky said, slipping her red satin jacket over her leotard and tights. "Lots of guys go through that office."

"But not like this one! He's got black hair and sparkling blue eyes."

"How tall is he?" Zan asked, unconsciously bending her knees to appear shorter.

"I couldn't tell, he was sitting down," Gwen replied. "But I'd say he was most definitely a sixth-grader." A worried look crossed her face. "Do I look OK?"

Gwen turned to face her reflection in the mirror. A short, chubby twelve-year-old with thick glasses and limp red hair stared back at her. "Why didn't someone tell me I looked like this?"

"Like what?" Rocky came over and stood behind her.

"This!" She pointed at her reflection. "I'm not leaving this dressing room until I lose fifty pounds."

"What are you getting all excited about?" Rocky asked. "He's probably somebody's brother here to pick her up."

Gwen sucked in her stomach as hard as she could and replied, "No, this boy is here to take dance lessons. He's wearing tights."

"Oooh, I want to look!" Mary Bubnik skipped over to the long black curtain that separated the dressing

2

room from the front lounge. She parted the curtain slightly and looked out.

A dark-haired boy was sitting quietly on the sofa by the receptionist's desk. He wore a white T-shirt over his black tights, with a pair of black dance shoes and white athletic socks.

"He's cute," Mary Bubnik giggled, and her blonde curls bobbed up and down.

"Cute?" Gwen said indignantly. "*Bambi* is cute. This boy is a major hunk."

"This I've got to see." Rocky joined Mary and peeked through the curtain at the boy in the lobby.

"Well, what do you think?" Gwen whispered.

"He's OK." Rocky shrugged her shoulders. "But if you've seen one boy, you've seen them all."

"You're just saying that 'cause you've got four brothers," Mary Bubnik said.

"Yeah, you hate boys," Gwen agreed. "You're always getting in fights with them at school."

Rocky, who's real name was Rochelle, had earned her nickname by being tough. She hated bullies, and any boy who teased her at school lived to regret it.

"Personally, I like boys," Mary Bubnik said with a smile. "Especially cute ones like him."

Just then Kathryn McGee stepped through the curtain. As she opened her mouth to say hello, Gwen blurted, "I saw him first!"

"Saw who?" McGee asked, taking a step back.

3

Gwen sighed exasperatedly. "The hunk in tights. He's sitting on the couch. You must have walked right by him."

McGee took her stocking cap off and flipped her chestnut braids over her shoulder. "Oh, you mean the boy Courtney's talking to?"

"What?" Gwen raced back to the curtain. Zan, McGee, and Mary Bubnik gathered around her, and they all peered through the little opening.

There, standing in a perfect fourth position, was Courtney Clay, their worst enemy. She was wearing a pretty wool coat with a fluffy fur collar over her perfect pink dance tights and black leotard. She pointed her leg out behind her in a perfect *arabesque* as she talked.

"Look at that Bunhead, posing like a dancer." Rocky had given Courtney and her friends the nickname "Bunheads" because they always wore their hair pulled back tightly in a bun. They thought they knew everything about ballet and were real snobs about it. "Who's she trying to kid, anyway?"

"That boy," Mary Bubnik groaned. "And it looks like he's falling for her in a big way."

The dark-haired boy was leaning forward on the sofa, smiling and nodding his head as he listened. Every once in a while he'd laugh at something she said, revealing the dimple in his cheek.

"I can't believe he'd fall for a Bunhead," Gwen

4

moaned, throwing herself dramatically across one of the wooden benches along the wall. Then she dug into her canvas dance bag and pulled out a handful of M&M's and popped them in her mouth. "It's just not fair."

"Geez Louise, Gwen," McGee said, tugging hard at the right leg of her faded tights, "he's just talking to her. He's not going to marry her." As she pulled on her tights, a run that had been working its way up her calf burst open and bared a wide patch of white kneecap.

"Very attractive," Courtney Clay said, stepping through the curtain into the dressing room. "Can you do that trick with your other leg?"

McGee, who usually had a stinging comeback for Courtney's snide remarks, just stared miserably at her tights. All she could think about was how she'd have to walk past that cute boy looking like a total slob.

"I told my mom to get me new tights," she grumbled. "I'm tired of hand-me-downs." Her two older sisters had worn those tights before her. The tights had been washed so many times that they were no longer pink but a drab gray.

Rocky, who had returned to the curtain to take another look at the new boy, announced suddenly, "Make way for the duck!"

She stepped back just as Page Tuttle swept into

5

the dressing room. The pretty blonde paraded past Rocky with her feet turned out in the telltale dancer's walk. Except for the color of her hair, Page might have been an identical copy of her best friend, Courtney Clay. She placed her dance bag on the dressing table and announced dramatically, "There's a *boy* in the lobby!"

Courtney, who had already removed her coat and was busy doing *pliés* and stretches to warm up, answered smugly, "I've already talked to him. He's going to be taking classes here."

"Really? How wonderful!" Page hung up her coat and promptly joined Courtney in her warm-ups. "This ballet school needs more male dancers. For partnering."

"Partnering?" Mary Bubnik repeated pleasantly. "You mean, like for square dancing?"

"Oh, *puh-leeze!*" Page rolled her eyes at Courtney, and the two girls snickered.

Zan put her hand on Mary Bubnik's arm. "Partnering is when a boy dances with a girl. You know, like when the Sugar Plum Fairy danced with the Cavalier in *The Nutcracker.*"

"Oh." Mary Bubnik nodded her head. "I remember."

"It will be so nice to have someone to dance with in our class," Courtney said, sliding down into a split.

Gwen, who had stepped behind the full-length mirror to change into her black leotard and tights, popped her head around the side. "They wouldn't put him in with us, would they?"

"Well, of course," Page replied. "Our class is for fifth- and sixth-graders. Where else do you think they'd put him?"

"In a boys' class," Mary Bubnik answered.

Gwen stepped out gingerly from behind the mirror. "I'm not leaping around dressed like this in front of a boy." She gestured at her leotard and made a face. It was too tight in the middle and made her look even pudgier than she was. "No way."

"Me, neither." McGee crossed her arms firmly across her chest.

Zan nodded her agreement. "Taking ballet can be embarrassing enough without having a boy staring at us." Zan was taller than every boy in the fifth grade at Stewart Elementary. She spent most of her time at school feeling like a too tall, clumsy giraffe. She didn't want her dance class to be the same way.

"I don't really care," Rocky announced. "He just better stay out of my way." She added a karate kick into the air for emphasis.

"Maybe we could ask him politely to go someplace else," Mary Bubnik suggested. The last thing she wanted was to have that cute boy watch her trip over her feet. Which she was certain to do because her ballet slippers were too big. Her mother had bought them a couple of sizes too large, hoping she'd grow into them.

7

"Maybe *you* could go someplace else," Courtney said with a sickeningly sweet smile. "Someplace far, far away. That would make everybody happy."

"Maybe you'd like your bun moved to the middle of your face," Rocky growled, springing to Mary Bubnik's defense.

Courtney turned pale, then answered back, "You wouldn't dare!"

Before Rocky could make a move, a girl with strawberry-blonde hair and big green eyes stuck her head through the gap in the curtain. "Excuse me, is this where we change if we're taking Miss Springer's class?"

Mary Bubnik answered first. "It sure is. Come on in."

No one said so, but they were all relieved that the newcomer had stopped a potential fight.

"My name's Mary Bubnik. What's yours?"

"Trisha Miller." The girl smiled shyly. "I just moved here."

Mary Bubnik flashed a big, friendly smile. "Me, too. My mom and I moved here from Oklahoma last fall. It's hard being new, isn't it?"

The girl nodded as she slipped off her coat. She was already wearing her leotard and tights. Trisha did a couple of stretches that quickly revealed that she knew what she was doing.

"Uh-oh," Rocky murmured to McGee, "another Bunhead."

8

Courtney watched the girl do her exercises and then smiled warmly. "I'm Courtney Clay. My mother is on the board of directors for the Deerfield Academy of Dance." She paused to let the new girl be suitably impressed by this information, then said, "I've trained for six years."

"So have I," Page Tuttle added, not to be outdone.

Trisha quickly plaited her red hair into one long braid down her back and said, "I've only studied for three, but I love it. I was afraid there wouldn't be a good dance school when we moved."

Courtney lifted her chin proudly. "The Academy is one of the best in all of Ohio."

Trisha smiled. "That's what I've heard."

The gang listened to their exchange with sinking hearts. Right now their dance class was split evenly down the middle. Half of the girls were like Courtney and Page — they were obsessed with ballet and despised any girl who wasn't. The other half were like Gwen and McGee. They were forced by their mothers to take dance. They didn't care for it much, but it was a good excuse to see their friends. Now it sounded like Trisha and the new boy would be joining Courtney and the Bunheads.

"We're going to be outnumbered," McGee whispered.

"What do you mean, we?" Gwen hissed back. "I'm not going into that class if *he's* going to be there."

"Want to bet?" Rocky said with a grin. She gestured toward the door, where Miss Delacorte, the aging receptionist for the Academy, had just popped her head into the room. She was wearing a red turban and a long red dress and heavy bracelets that jangled from her thin arms.

"What are you girls do-ink in here?" the woman asked in her thick Russian accent. "Your teacher is waiting. Class is about to begin." She clapped her hands together. "Hurry, hurry!"

Courtney quickly applied some pale pink lipstick and skipped toward the curtain. Page and the new girl followed her out the door. "This should be fun," Courtney trilled.

"A laugh a minute," Rocky grumbled as she and the others trudged reluctantly behind them.

Gwen made one last effort to suck in her stomach and wheezed, "I can't wait."

Chapter Two

Several young dancers were already at the ballet *barre* warming up when the girls entered the brightly lit studio. Rocky led the gang over to their usual spot on the far side of the room. Courtney and Page went immediately to the front of the class nearest the piano. The new boy and girl were left standing in the center of the room, looking slightly embarrassed.

Their teacher, Annie Springer, waited patiently for them to take their places. She was dressed in a long-sleeved leotard with a short black dance skirt wrapped around her tiny waist. Her dark brown hair was swept into a pretty bun at the base of her neck, and she looked every inch the leading ballerina that she was.

11

"I'm glad everyone could make it today," Annie announced. "We have some fresh faces in our class." She smiled warmly at the two newcomers. "Before we begin our warm-ups, why don't you tell us your names and a little bit about yourselves?"

The new girl's face turned bright red. "My name is Trisha Miller," she said quietly, "and I just moved here from New York City."

"New York?" Courtney Clay was visibly impressed. "Did you study dance there?"

Trisha nodded. "At the American Ballet Theatre."

"Oh, I'm green with envy," Annie Springer said.

"Me, too," Page Tuttle sighed.

"What's the American Ballet Theatre?" Mary Bubnik whispered to McGee.

"Must be some famous company in New York," McGee whispered back.

Zan nodded. "And Mikhail Baryshnikov is the director of it. He's truly wonderful, the best dancer in the world."

Annie Springer clasped her hands together in front of her. "Welcome to our class, Trisha. I hope you'll be able to tell us a few wonderful stories about life in the ballet world of New York."

Trisha smiled shyly and stared down at her feet.

"I hope she's not a show-off," Rocky muttered.

"She doesn't act like it," Zan said. "She seems awfully nice."

"Wait'll those Bunheads get a hold of her," Gwen

12

grumbled. "She'll turn into a snob, just like the rest of them."

"I hope not," Mary Bubnik whispered.

Now it was the boy's turn. Every girl in the class held her breath as they waited to hear his name. He looked at the teacher with his serious blue eyes and declared, "I'm Zachary Smith. Most people call me Zach."

A soft murmur went around the room as everyone repeated his name.

"Zachary-Thackary," Rocky sang mockingly under her breath, and McGee gave her a nudge with her elbow.

"I've been studying ballet at the YMCA," Zach continued, "but the classes there are only for beginners. So my teacher thought I should continue my classes here."

"We're glad you did," Annie smiled. "It's nice to have a boy in our class."

"What's so nice about it?" Gwen grumbled as she exhaled a great gasp of breath. She had been concentrating so hard on sucking in her stomach that she felt dizzy.

"It'll give you girls a chance to learn how to dance with a partner." Suddenly Annie snapped her fingers. "I've got an idea!"

She hurried over to Mrs. Bruce, the elderly accompanist, and whispered something in her ear. The old lady smiled and thumbed quickly through her

13

sheet music. Annie turned and announced, "Because it's still winter and Lake Deerfield is completely frozen over, I thought it would be appropriate for us to dance to *'Les Patineurs,'* which is French for 'The Skaters.' "

Courtney and several other girls clapped their hands together in delight.

"I don't like the sound of this," Gwen grumbled.

"I do," McGee replied with a grin. She spent most of her time after school on the ice, practicing with her hockey team, the Fairview Express. The idea of pretending to dance on ice suited her just fine.

Annie moved to the piano, placed her hand on it, using it like a ballet *barre,* and said, "First let's do some warm-ups, and then we'll pair up."

"Pair up?" Gwen repeated. "I can barely dance by myself. What am I going to do in a pair?"

"Who could they possibly pair me with?" Zan moaned as they started their *pliés.* "I tower over everyone here."

"I think you and Zachary might be the same height," McGee teased.

"Oh, don't say that!" Zan's knees locked at the thought of dancing with a boy. She turned to Rocky, who was still doing warm-ups behind her, and begged, "Please, Rocky, be my partner."

Rocky shrugged. "Sure."

As the girls dutifully went through their warm-ups, Miss Springer walked around the room from dancer

14

to dancer, instructing them to pull in their stomachs, or turn out their feet and straighten their knees. As they practiced, each girl kept one eye glued to the big mirror covering the front wall of the studio. They were all watching Zach's every move.

"He's really good," Mary Bubnik gushed over Rocky's shoulder.

"Really?" Rocky replied as she executed a high kick called a *grand battement* in the air in front of her. "I didn't notice."

Annie clapped her hands to end the warm-up period. "Now, form two lines, and we'll pair up in couples for the dance of the skaters."

Zach stepped away from the *barre* and was the first in one of the lines. Courtney and Page raced to be in the front of the other line so they could be his partner.

"I was here first," Courtney said, giving Page a gentle shove out of the way.

Page replied firmly through clenched teeth, "You were not." She nudged Courtney with her elbow and moved back to the front of the line. "And don't push me!"

"Who's pushing who?" Courtney demanded, grabbing Page's arm and pulling her back behind her.

"Cut it out!" Page yanked her arm away from Courtney. The rest of class watched in amazement as the two girls jostled each other to be first.

15

"I can't believe the Bunheads are fighting," McGee said with glee. "Any bets on who'll win?"

"I don't know," Mary Bubnik said with a giggle. "Courtney looks madder than a wet hen."

The two Bunheads were standing nose to nose, glaring fiercely into each other's face. "You seem to forget," Courtney hissed, "that my mother is on the board of this ballet company."

"So?" Page crossed her arms stubbornly. "She may be on the board, but that has nothing to do with this ballet class. The best dancer should go first. And I'm the best."

Courtney's eyes widened. "You are not! I am."

Courtney and Page were so busy fighting that they didn't notice that the line had formed without them. Trisha the new girl was at the front, and the rest of the class fell in behind her. Annie moved between the two lines assigning partners. She finally stopped by the two girls and announced, "And Courtney and Page — you two will dance together."

When Courtney realized that someone else would be dancing with Zach she hissed, "You'll regret this, Page Tuttle."

Annie moved to the front of the room. "Now the steps we're going to dance together are simple. It'll be just like skating. First we slide on our right foot, and hop for two counts in an *arabesque,* then we do the same thing with our left foot. Then we add

16

a simple waltz step, like this." She demonstrated the movements down the center of the room. "One, two, three — down, up, up."

As the class watched her waltz around the room with an imaginary partner, Mary Bubnik groaned. "I hope you remember the steps, McGee, because I can't."

"Piece of cake," McGee's green eyes sparkled. This dance would be a cinch, and she'd impress Zach with how good an athlete she was.

Annie gestured to Mrs. Bruce to begin the music, and the accompanist responded with the first few chords on the piano. Zach and Trisha were the first to dance across the room. They were hesitant at first, and Rocky snickered loudly at the couple. But, after a few steps, they loosened up and began to work together as a team.

"That looks so romantic," Mary Bubnik sighed as the pair swept by them. Gwen nodded her head unconsciously. She wished Zach were dancing with her instead of the new girl.

Next McGee and Mary Bubnik moved onto the floor. "Now, remember," McGee whispered under her breath, "slide on your right foot first."

Mary Bubnik nodded and promptly began the dance on her left foot. "Oops! I always get right and left confused." McGee shot her a dirty look and yanked Mary in the right direction. That made Mary

17

Bubnik forget the rest of the steps, and she began to giggle hysterically out of embarrassment. McGee tried her hardest to get through the dance without looking too silly but, with a giggling maniac trotting along beside her, that was impossible.

The moment they reached the other side of the room, she let go of Mary's hands in disgust. "Geez Louise, Mary, can't you ever get *anything* right?"

A hurt look crossed Mary's face for a second, then she forced an apologetic smile. "Gosh, I'm so sorry, McGee, I think having *him* here made me get all nervous."

Rocky and Zan came next. Zan kept trying to hide behind Rocky instead of dancing beside her. Their feet got tangled up and Zan stepped on the heel of Rocky's shoe. "Whooaaaa!" Rocky yelled as her foot jerked out of her ballet slipper.

"Are you all right?" Annie called.

"We're fine," Rocky replied, hastily grabbing her shoe. Then she turned to Zan and grumbled, "Next time, try dancing on your own feet."

"Sorry," Zan murmured softly, but Rocky had already stalked away from her to sit with McGee at the back of the room.

Gwen's partner was Alice Wescott, the youngest of the Bunheads. They moved across the floor, with Alice doing her best to show off. When she hopped, she leaped as high as she could into the air. Gwen, on the other hand, didn't want her tummy to jiggle when she jumped, so she never let her feet leave the floor.

"They look like they're in a tug-o'-war," McGee cracked.

Moments later Gwen joined the rest of the girls and gasped, "I'm glad that's over!" She shook her head emphatically. "Next time she mentions partners, I'm out of here."

Rocky nudged Gwen with her elbow. "Get a load of the Bunheads."

Page and Courtney were dancing serenely down the center of the dance floor. Each girl had her own version of a mysterious ballerina smile on her face; her eyes glazed over with a wistful far-off look. They were trying so hard to impress Zach that they weren't watching where they were going. Everyone saw the collision coming before they did, and the room shouted as one, "Look out!"

But it was too late. Page and Courtney plowed into the piano which rolled and nearly knocked Mrs. Bruce off her bench. The music stopped and Annie rushed to see if the girls were hurt.

"I'm fine," Courtney said, trying to rise above it all. "I guess Page wasn't watching where she was going."

Page gasped in dismay. "You're the one that dragged me into the piano. Now I'm going to have a big bruise on my leg." She bent over and gently kneaded the spot where the grand piano caught her in the thigh.

"Oh, poor baby," Courtney said sarcastically. They glared at each other angrily.

"Wow! If they're trying to impress Zach," McGee said, "they're certainly doing a lousy job of it."

"Yeah, isn't it great?" Gwen giggled, relieved that someone else had looked like an idiot in front of Zach. Mary Bubnik and Zan both nodded in agreement.

Fortunately their hour was nearly up so everyone was spared the embarrassment of having to do the dance again. Miss Springer called the group in a circle around her. "Two weeks from today is Valentine's Day. Since it falls on a Saturday, the academy has decided to have a party for the students with — "

"Cookies?" Gwen piped up.

Annie laughed. "Yes, with cookies and punch."

"And valentines?" Alice Wescott asked, casting a dewy-eyed smile in Zach's direction.

"Well, sure," Annie replied. "If you'd like."

There was a chorus of "Yea!" from the girls in the class.

"Great! Then that's it for today." Miss Springer swept into a low curtsy that the group imitated. "Be careful in the snow, and I'll see you next week."

Before Zach could reach the door, he was surrounded by most of the girls in the class. They were all giggling and talking at once.

After Zach left, Mary skipped over to Rocky. "I think he is the cutest boy I have ever met."

Rocky stared her straight in the eye and said, "Barf-o-Rama." Then she turned on her heel and marched into the dressing room.

Courtney was already there, telling Alice Wescott, "I have the perfect valentine to give Zach. I saw it at the mall last week and bought it, just in case I found somebody special."

Rocky threw her arms up in the air. "Has everyone gone boy crazy, or what?"

Just then Gwen stuck her head in the dressing room. "Anyone want to get a Coke before we go home?"

"Yeah," McGee shouted. "I'm dying of thirst."

"Me, too," Mary Bubnik chirped.

"Count me in," Rocky was relieved that they had stopped talking about the new boy.

As they all filed out of the dressing room and down the stairs of Hillberry Hall, Gwen whispered, "That way we can talk about Zach and no one will hear us."

Chapter Three

"Hi, Hi!" Gwen shouted as the five girls charged into Hi Lo's Pizza and Chinese Food To Go. The tiny restaurant was tucked between a jewelry store and a loan office across the street from the Deerfield Academy.

"Greetings and salutations, my little friends," Mr. Lo called out with a smile. His face creased into a rippling sea of tiny lines. "What can I get for my favorite ballerinas today?"

"I'll have a Cherry Coke and an order of fries," Gwen said, hopping onto one of the six leather stools that lined the counter.

The rest of the girls ordered Cokes, and Hi bowed.

"Your wish is my command." As he disappeared into the kitchen to get their drinks, the girls huddled together to talk about Zach.

"My main problem is my height," Zan complained. "I mean, do I just tower over him?"

"Of course, you don't," Mary Bubnik reassured her. Then she added truthfully, "Not much."

McGee held up one of her braids and grimaced. "Does my hair look ridiculous, or what?"

Rocky threw up her hands in exasperation. "If you ask me, I think you're all ridiculous."

"Did you see the dimple in his cheek?" Mary Bubnik sighed.

"I like his deep blue eyes," Zan said. "They were sort of sad. I wonder if he has a tragic past."

"Oh, give me a break," Rocky groaned, spinning away from them on her stool.

"He's such a good dancer," McGee mused. "I'll bet he's a good athlete, too. Do you think he likes ice hockey?"

Mary Bubnik put her head in her hands. "Why did I have to laugh like that? He must think I'm a complete loony."

"But you are," McGee replied, trying to keep a straight face.

"Really?" Mary's bright blue eyes widened in horror. "Do you guys really think I'm loony?"

"I'd say you were a goonie," Gwen quipped.

"No," Zan said thoughtfully, "just a dingbat."

"Definitely," Rocky agreed, "with geek-like tendencies."

As Mr. Lo set their orders in front of them, Mary demanded, "Hi, do you think I'm a geeky, goonie, loony dingbat?"

"Well, let me see," he replied. "If that means you're a nice, friendly girl with a lovely smile, yes."

Rocky took a sip of her Coke. "What it means is that she's boy crazy."

"Boy crazy!" Mary Bubnik repeated indignantly. "I am not."

"Are, too," Rocky shot back.

"Am not!"

"What's this about a crazy boy?" Hi interrupted.

Before anyone could answer, the little bell over the door tinkled and Annie Springer stepped into the restaurant.

"Annie!" Gwen gasped. "What are you doing here?"

"I've come for my lunch," she replied pleasantly. "Are you girls waiting for your moms?"

They nodded. Hi reached below the counter and pulled out a little white box with metal handles and a covered styrofoam cup. "Here you are, Miss Annie. One hot tea, and an order of steamed vegetables, to go."

"Thanks, Hi." As Mr. Lo was ringing up her bill, she leaned against the counter and sighed.

"What's the matter?" Zan asked softly.

24

The ballerina looked up at her in surprise, as if she'd forgotten the girls were there, then shook her head. "It's nothing," she replied, "I'm just a little tired. I've got another long rehearsal today." Mr. Lo handed the ballerina her change, and she gathered up her dinner. "Bye, girls. See you next week."

No one said a word as they watched her leave.

"Geez Louise," McGee said. "She seems so sad."

"I wonder what's the matter?" Zan asked.

"She comes in here three times a week," Hi said, "and always orders the same thing."

"Where does she take it?" Gwen asked.

"Back to the studio. She teaches classes during the day, and rehearses with the ballet company at night."

"Doesn't she date, or anything?" Rocky asked.

Mr. Lo shook his head. "Who knows? With a schedule like that, when would she find the time?"

"They must give her *some* days off," Gwen reasoned.

"And she *must* have a boyfriend," Mary Bubnik added.

"I'm pretty certain she doesn't," Mr. Lo said. "Sometimes at nights, when I'm closing up, I see her waiting for the bus alone."

"How tragic!" Zan said, her large brown eyes misting over.

"She must be so lonely!" Mary said.

"It's not fair," McGee muttered. "Annie's too nice not to have a boyfriend."

25

"If she doesn't have time to go out," Rocky said, "she probably just hasn't had a chance to meet any guys."

"That's so awful!"

They all slumped down on the counter, horrified at the thought of their lovely teacher pining away in loneliness.

Suddenly Mary Bubnik murmured, "Somebody should help her."

"Like who?" Rocky said.

"Like us," Gwen declared.

"What can we do?"

"Find her a boyfriend," McGee answered.

"And we should do it by Valentine's Day," Zan said. "Otherwise, she'll spend it all alone, wishing someone would give her flowers."

"We need to find someone who'll send her chocolates," Gwen said.

"And take her to a hockey game," McGee added.

"And then out to a fabulous dinner," Gwen continued.

"In a beautiful evening gown," Rocky chimed in.

"Then they'll drive out to Lake Deerfield," Zan said, "where they'll look up at the stars, and he'll read her poetry."

"Then he'll take her in his arms and — " Mary Bubnik paused dramatically.

"Kiss her!" The girls erupted into gales of laughter.

"Then It's settled," Gwen said. "We're going to find Annie a boyfriend."

"By Valentine's Day," Zan added.

"Or else," Rocky finished, crossing her arms.

"Listen," McGee warned, "we'd better keep this a secret. If Annie found out we were trying to get her a boyfriend, she'd probably tell us to forget it."

"And then she'd stay all lonely and forlorn," Zan said.

"Forlorn?" McGee repeated. "What's that mean?"

"Desperate," Gwen explained.

Rocky and McGee nodded. "That's Annie."

"Then we have to give our plan a secret name," Zan said.

"I've got it!" Rocky exclaimed. "When my dad goes on maneuvers with the Air Force, they always use a code name, like Operation Mad Dog."

Gwen looked at her skeptically. "I don't think Operation Mad Dog really fits our situation."

"I don't mean for us to call it *that*," Rocky said quickly. "But how does Operation Annie sound?"

"I like it!" Zan took out her lavender pad and wrote the name down on a clean sheet of paper. "Now we need a code name for ourselves."

"How about the Detectives?" Mary Bubnik suggested.

"Naw." McGee shook her head. "We're not solving any mystery."

"How about the Spies?" Rocky suggested.

"We're trying to *keep* a secret," Gwen pointed out, "Not *steal* one."

"What exactly *are* we trying to do?" Mary Bubnik asked.

"Find the perfect boy," McGee explained, "and make him fall in love with Annie."

"I've got it!" Zan cried suddenly. "We should call ourselves the Cupids."

"Cupids?" Rocky looked at her dubiously. "Why Cupids?"

"In Greek mythology Cupid went around shooting golden arrows at people and making them fall madly in love with each other."

"Oh, that's so sweet," Mary Bubnik giggled.

"I like the arrow part," Rocky nodded approvingly.

"OK," McGee said. "We're the Cupids."

"Now I think we should have a meeting this week," Zan said, "to plan our strategy."

"Why don't we have it at my house on the air base?" Rocky suggested. "My dad's out of town, and it's just my mom and me." She paused and added, "And my four dumb brothers."

"Gee, I've never been on an air force base before," Mary Bubnik said. "Is it scary?"

"Why would it be scary?" Rocky asked.

"Well, all those guns and planes with bombs."

"You never see any of that stuff," Rocky said. "Sometimes planes fly overhead and make a lot of

28

noise, but mostly you just see guys in uniforms, and lots of houses that all look exactly alike."

"Hey, my mom can drive us there," Mary Bubnik announced.

"Great," McGee said. "That solves our transportation problem."

"We need a secret sign," Zan said quietly. "One that lets each of us know that we want to talk about Operation Annie."

"How about this?" Rocky said. She made a fist and pounded it against her chest. "I saw some gladiators do that in a movie, and it was really cool."

"I don't know," McGee said, "it's a little strong."

"Let's cross our hands over our hearts," Gwen suggested.

"Oooh, that's romantic," Mary Bubnik sighed, folding her hands over her heart. The others did the same just as Mr. Lo came out of the kitchen.

"What's the matter, my friends?" he asked, seeing their solemn faces. "Are you still upset about crazy boys?"

"No," Rocky replied firmly. "We have much more important things to think about."

"And we're sworn to secrecy," Zan whispered.

"I see."

"We'll tell you all about it when our mission is accomplished." Rocky looked up at the dragon-shaped clock over the counter. "I don't know about you guys, but if I'm not home by sixteen hundred

29

hours, I'll be confined to quarters for the rest of the weekend."

The girls all knew what Rocky meant. Her dad was a sergeant in the Air Force and ran his household just like a military unit. "Sixteen hundred hours" meant four o'clock and "confined to quarters" meant having to stay in your room.

They paid for their drinks and said good-bye. Rocky led the way out the door. As soon as they were on the sidewalk, she stopped in her tracks and the others crashed into her back.

"There he is!" Rocky exclaimed.

"Who?" McGee asked.

"Him." Rocky pointed across the street. Zachary Smith was walking nonchalantly down the sidewalk, swinging his canvas sports bag by the handle.

"I thought you didn't like boys," McGee said.

"I don't," Rocky replied. "I just know you girls are going to make idiots of yourselves again, and then he'll see me with you, and think I'm just as big a geek as the rest of you."

"We're not going to make any big deal out of seeing some boy," Gwen declared.

"After all," Zan said, "we have Operation Annie to think about."

"And besides, only Bunheads would act like that," McGee added. "Right, Mary?"

Mary Bubnik wasn't listening. McGee tapped her on the shoulder and repeated, "Right, Mary?"

Suddenly Mary Bubnik squealed, "He's looking at me!" She flapped her arms up and down and bellowed, "Hi, Zach!"

Gwen, Zan, and McGee hopped up and down, waving furiously. Gwen's blue dance bag fell to the ground, and Twinkies, M&M's, and two cans of diet soda rolled out onto the sidewalk.

Rocky flattened herself against the plate glass window of Hi Lo's place and muttered, "This isn't happening. Those are not my friends. When I open my eyes, they'll be gone."

Chapter Four

"Mom!" Rocky yelled from the kitchen, "will you tell Joey and David to quit eating the snacks I fixed?"

"Joseph! David! Leave your sister alone," Mrs. Garcia shouted from the other end of the house.

Her mother's command didn't phaze Rocky's brothers one bit, particularly Joey. He was the closest to her in age and was always tormenting her — at school, on the bus, and at home. Joey held a corn chip right in front of her face and loudly bit it in half.

"You're going to get it," Rocky said, pointing the cheese cutter at him. "Just wait till you try to have some friends over and see what I do."

"Oh, I'm *really* scared" — Joey knocked his

knees together exaggeratedly — "I'm shakin' in my shoes."

"That's it. I've *had* it!" Rocky marched down the hall to her bedroom and slammed the door behind her. "Nothing is working out," she groaned as she threw herself on her bed. It had been like this all day long. Her four brothers seemed determined to make her life miserable and her party a disaster.

There was a soft knock on her bedroom door.

"Come on in, Mom." Rocky knew it was her mother because none of her brothers would have bothered to knock.

Mrs. Garcia sat on the edge of her bed and smoothed a strand of Rocky's wild hair. "Is everything ready for the meeting?"

"I don't know." Rocky had her face buried in her pillow, and her words were muffled. "I hate being the only girl in this family. They're just awful to me."

"I know it can be tough some times," her mother said, "but you know that, deep down inside, your brothers love you."

"They sure have a funny way of showing it." Rocky sat up and hugged the pillow to her stomach. "David and Joey ate one whole bag of corn chips and the entire bowl of dip. Michael scribbled all over my favorite notepad, and Jay invited that weird friend of his over to listen to music. *Loud* music." Rocky raised her head to look at her mother. "They promised they'd leave me alone today. Now they're just going to embarrass me."

"There's no reason to get upset," Mrs. Garcia said soothingly, patting her daughter on the shoulder. "I've got an extra bag of chips in the pantry, we'll take a yellow pad out of your dad's desk for you to write on, and I'll talk to Jay and the boys and ask them to go to a friend's house till dinner. OK?"

Rocky nodded and wiped her nose with her hand. "Thanks, Mom."

"Now, come on and let's make sure we have enough sodas for everyone." Mrs. Garcia led Rocky down the hall of their neat four-bedroom home. It was the largest type of house you could get on their side of the air base and usually reserved for officers with more seniority than Sergeant Garcia. But since there were seven in their family, the Garcias qualified. It still wasn't big enough, as far as Rocky was concerned.

"Oh, Mom, look!" Rocky stopped as they passed the door to the living room. "Michael left his smelly socks on the floor again." Michael was the second oldest and the biggest slob of all the Garcia kids.

"I'll have him pick them up."

"And what's that?" Rocky shrieked, pointing to the pile of clean clothes neatly stacked by the dryer in the kitchen. "Boy's underwear? Oh, Mom, that'll gross everyone out!"

34

"I'm sure your friends have seen underwear before."

"Yeah," David said, racing in from the dining room. He grabbed a pair of boxer shorts and put them on his head.

Usually the goofy things David did made her laugh, but not today. Today she was having her friends over to her house for the first time, and Rocky wanted to make a good impression.

Joey saw what David was doing and put a pair of underwear on his head, too. The two of them danced around the kitchen, pretending to be swamis from India. Rocky sank down into a chair and groaned, "This is going to be a total disaster."

At the same moment Rocky was trying to cope with her brothers, Mrs. Bubnik was attempting to enter the main gate of Curtiss-Dobbs Air Force Base with a car full of girls.

"Hey, Mom," Mary Bubnik yelled, "that sign says guests must use the right lane."

"Right lane?" Mrs. Bubnik repeated. "but I'm already here in the left. There's a whole line of cars in that lane. How do I get over there?"

"Signal," Gwen called from the backseat.

"That's easy for you to say," Mrs. Bubnik murmured. She tried flicking on the turn signal but nothing happened. "Oh, shoot! It's on the blink again."

The old green Volvo was always breaking down,

but neither Mary nor her mother could bear the thought of selling it. Their car, which they'd named Mr. Toad, was such a part of their family that they had simply learned to cope with the car's tendency to break down when you least expected it.

"Mary," Mrs. Bubnik said, "stick your head out the window, and see if someone in that lane will let us in."

Mary Bubnik rolled down her window and waved at the cars in the right lane. The line didn't budge. "Nothing's happening."

"Try this." Gwen rolled down her window in the backseat and shouted, "OK, everybody, act sick!"

Gwen, McGee, and Zan stuck their heads out of the back window with their hands over their mouths. McGee mouthed the words, "I think I'm going to throw up!" at the driver next to them, and he immediately slammed on his brakes.

"OK, Mom," Mary called, "you're in!"

Mrs. Bubnik eased into the right lane and pulled up to the checkpoint where a big white sign proclaimed Welcome to Curtiss-Dobbs Air Force Base. She pulled into a slot marked Guests Only.

The two men in smart blue uniforms were talking to the driver in front of them. Their blue pants were tucked neatly inside their shiny black boots. They had on white gloves, white helmets, and white belts strapped around their hips.

Mrs. Bubnik checked her reflection in the rearview

36

mirror and licked one finger to smooth the right side of her blonde hair. "I think men in uniform are so attractive," she said, digging in her purse for her lipstick and quickly applying the rosy color to her lips. "How does that look? Did I smear it?"

"It looks just fine, Mom." Mary Bubnik couldn't help smiling. Ever since her parents had divorced, her mother had completely avoided meeting any men. She had hated it when Mary even mentioned the word *date*. It was good to see her taking an interest in guys again.

Zan looked at the soldiers and gasped. "They've got guns," she whispered. "What should we do?"

"I don't know," McGee answered. "I've never been on a military base before."

"What if they think we're spies, trying to steal their secret weapons?" Mary Bubnik giggled nervously.

"Then they'll just take us to the brig," McGee said, remembering that word from an old war movie she'd seen on television. "And we'll be forced to do KP for the rest of our lives."

"KP?"

"Kitchen Police," Gwen explained. "That means doing the dirty dishes and peeling onions for ever and ever."

The two guards stepped back and crisply saluted the car in front of them as it drove onto the base. Then one of them motioned Mrs. Bubnik to pull forward.

"Oh, dear," Mrs. Bubnik said, stuffing her lipstick back in the purse. "Here we go."

"Now, remember," Zan whispered to the rest of the girls, "no matter what they ask, don't tell them about you-know-what."

Mary Bubnik cocked her head in confusion and McGee mouthed, "Operation Annie."

"Oh!" Mary Bubnik nodded. Then to show that she understood, she crossed her hands over her heart in their secret sign. The other girls did the same.

"Where are you headed, ma'am?" the guard asked as he leaned on the car and peered in the window.

To everyone's surprise Mrs. Bubnik saluted! This sent the girls in the backseat into gales of laughter. Mary tried to stifle her giggling by burying her face in her hands. Mrs. Bubnik's face immediately turned beet-red. "Uh, hello, I'm looking for, um . . . you see, they're expecting us to . . . they live on — oh, dear, where did I put the address?"

The guard exchanged a look with his partner, who was busy writing down the license plate number on a clipboard.

Mrs. Bubnik rummaged through her purse looking for the address. She emptied the contents onto the front seat beside her. Kleenex, change, several car keys, a compact, a roll of Lifesavers, and her billfold tumbled out and spilled onto the floor. This, of course, made the girls in the backseat laugh even harder.

The guard looked back at them and frowned. "What's the joke?" They immediately stopped laughing.

"Me," Mrs. Bubnik replied. "I'm the joke." Now she was going through her pockets. "I can't seem to find anything." Then she started giggling, which sounded like an echo of her daughter's laugh. "It's always like this. I don't know how I find my way out of my house."

The more Mrs. Bubnik laughed, the sterner the guard looked.

"That guy hasn't smiled once," Gwen whispered through clenched teeth. "What is he, a robot?"

"I don't know, but he makes me terribly nervous," Zan replied. "I feel like we're going into a prison."

"Mom, did you look in the glove compartment?" Mary finally suggested.

Mrs. Bubnik flipped open the little compartment and a slip of paper fell out. "Wouldn't you know it? Here it is!"

The guard took the paper in his white-gloved hands, and his face spread into a slow smile. "Oh, Sergeant Garcia? Why didn't you say so? He's with security, too. I know where he lives."

He told her the directions as he filled out a guest

pass. Then he handed it to her and said, "Put this on your dashboard, and be sure to return it when you leave the base."

"Yes, sir!"

The guard snapped to attention and saluted. Then, with an elaborate hand signal, he gestured for Mrs. Bubnik to enter the base.

"He looks like a cheerleader," McGee said.

"You mean, a grimleader," Gwen cracked. "That guy doesn't know the meaning of the word *cheer*."

"They must be told to look serious," Zan said. "To scare enemies away."

"Well, he certainly scared me," Mrs. Bubnik admitted. "I hope he's not the one I have to talk to when I leave."

She followed the guard's directions and soon the green Volvo was rolling down Patterson Drive. Little streets lined with tiny houses in pastel colors branched off the main avenue. Each house was the same size as the one beside it. They were either gray, pink, blue, or white, with a carport and a clothesline in the backyard.

"Boy, all these houses look alike," Mary marveled. "I wonder how Rocky is able to recognize hers."

"Street name and number," Gwen answered logically. "But that's about it."

Mrs. Bubnik pulled to a halt in front of a light-gray house with neat white trim. She peered through

40

the windshield at the number above the door. "Do you think this is it?"

At that moment the front door burst open and two boys with boxer shorts on their heads charged into the front yard. Right behind them was Rocky, doing a flying karate kick, and shouting, "You're going to get it!"

The girls smiled at each other. "Yes, this is it."

Chapter Five

"Let's hold our meeting in the den," Rocky said once the gang was all inside the house. "Hopefully, we'll get some privacy there."

"Now you girls enjoy yourselves," Mrs. Garcia called after them as Rocky led them off down the hall. "Rosie and I will be having a cup of coffee here in the kitchen if you need anything."

McGee grabbed Mary Bubnik by the arm and whispered, "I didn't know your mom's name was Rosie."

"Oh, yeah," Mary Bubnik replied. "It's short for Rosamond, but everybody just calls her Rosie."

McGee chuckled and Mary asked, "What's so funny about her name?"

McGee shook her head, still grinning. "Doesn't it always strike you as funny when you hear someone call your mom by her real name? I mean, my mom's always just Mom to me. Half the time I think they're talking about someone else when I hear people ask for Norma."

"Is that your mom's name?" Gwen demanded.

McGee nodded.

"Gee," Gwen said, "I never knew that."

Halfway down the corridor they passed the bathroom door. McGee noticed a piece of paper tacked on it, with a neatly printed list of names.

"What's this?" McGee read the top of the page. "G.H.P. number six."

"G.H.P. stands for Garcia Household Procedure," Rocky said. "My dad's got them posted all over the house."

"What's it for?" Mary Bubnik asked.

"This one lists the order we're to use the bathroom in the morning."

"Geez Louise," McGee said. "You have to have an order?"

Rocky shrugged. "You better believe it. There are seven people in our family and only one bathroom to go around."

"Look, here's another one," Gwen said, pointing to the piece of paper posted by the sliding doors leading into the den. "G.H.P. number seven. Viewing privileges."

Rocky smiled. "That's for the TV. Each of us gets a certain day of the week where we get to choose one show that we want to watch. Then the next week Dad assigns us a new day."

"What if your favorite show doesn't play on your night?" Gwen asked logically.

"That's when the trading starts," Rocky replied with a grin. "Like, if I want to watch a show on David's night, then I either give him my night, or I offer to do his chores for that day, or week."

"What if he doesn't want to trade?" McGee asked.

"Then I'm out of luck." Rocky shrugged.

Mary Bubnik shook her head. "That's amazing. My mom and I have never used a list for anything."

"Not even for groceries?" Gwen asked.

"Well, she used to make up grocery lists but she always forgot them on the way to the store, so finally she just gave up."

"Boy, my dad has a list for *everything,*" Rocky said. "He even draws up a seating plan for us to use when we go on long trips in the van." Rocky shrugged and shook her head. "I guess it's his military training."

"Does he make you march in formation and salute?" Zan asked, looking at a portrait of the family on the wall. Sergeant Garcia stood in the back with two of the boys standing at attention on either side. Rocky and her mother sat in two chairs in the front The whole family looked terribly stiff and formal.

"No, he's not that strict, really," Rocky said with a chuckle. "His bark's a lot worse than his bite."

"Is he here?" McGee whispered, looking from side to side.

"No, remember? I told you he was going to be away with his unit."

The group all breathed a sigh of relief as they entered the den.

A lean teenager dressed in jeans and a Cincinnati Bengals football jersey was sitting on the couch with his feet up, watching television.

"Michael!" Rocky exclaimed, folding her arms across her chest. "Mom said you were going to go to a friend's house."

"Oh, really?" Michael picked up a piece of popcorn from the bowl on the coffee table, tossed it in the air, and caught it in his mouth.

"Yes, really." Rocky glared at him with all her might.

"Well, looks like I changed my plans." Michael smiled innocently at his sister, then leaped to his feet. "Hey, what is this, a Brownie meeting?"

"Michael! These are my friends," Rocky said exasperatedly. "I told you a million times already."

Michael grinned. "Just kidding. Come on, introduce me."

"Gwen, Mary, Zan, McGee," Rocky said between clenched teeth. "This is my slobby, jerky brother Mike. He's a freshman in high school, but he doesn't act like it."

Gwen and Mary Bubnik both giggled shyly. "Hi, Mike."

"Hey, are we having a party?" another brother called from the doorway. "Why didn't anyone tell me?"

Rocky spun to face him. "Because you're not invited, Jay, that's why."

"He's *really* cute," Mary Bubnik whispered to Zan, who nodded in agreement. Jay had dark, curly hair like Rocky but his eyes were a pretty shade of green. He had a square jaw and was at least six feet tall. Mary figured he must be Rocky's oldest brother, the one at Deerfield College.

"Jay, please, go away," Rocky pleaded as she tried to push him out of the room. "We have some important matters to discuss."

"Sure." Jay strode past her and dug his hand in the bowl of popcorn.

"Jay!" Rocky swiped at him. "That's for my friends."

At that moment, David and Joey charged into the room, tossing a basketball between them.

"That does it!" Rocky shouted finally. "We're getting out of here."

She yanked the popcorn bowl out of Michael's

hand and gave it to Gwen. Then she picked up the bag of potato chips and dip and said, "Everybody grab a can of soda pop. We're leaving."

McGee could tell by the determined look in Rocky's eyes that she meant business. She motioned to the others and they obediently followed Rocky out the sliding glass doors onto the patio. Rocky led them through the ankle-deep snow in the backyard to a solitary oak tree.

"Where are we going?" Gwen huffed as she labored to keep up with Rocky.

"To my tree house. Those twerps won't bother us there."

"I don't blame them," McGee grumbled. "It's cold out here."

"There are blankets in the fort."

Gwen stopped at the bottom of the tree and stared up at the barren branches overhead. A square wooden structure rested between the fork of the trunk and two large branches about ten feet overhead. "How are we supposed to get up there? Fly?"

"We're going to have to climb," Rocky said.

"Climb? But I can't," Gwen protested. "I'm holding the popcorn."

"Then I'll carry it," Rocky said, taking it from Gwen.

"I don't know about this, y'all," Mary Bubnik said in a tiny voice. "I have never climbed up a big old tree like this in my whole life."

"That makes two of us," Gwen muttered.

47

"Aw, come on, it's easy," McGee said. She pointed to a row of little wooden steps nailed up the side of the tree trunk. "Look, we even have a ladder."

"I think I should tell everyone that I'm terribly afraid of heights," Zan said in a shaky voice.

"Let's get one thing straight," Rocky declared, setting the bowl of chips on the ground. "If we don't go up there, then we'll never be able to work on Operation Annie, and this whole visit will be a total bust."

"But couldn't we just go to your room?" Gwen suggested.

"No," Rocky said flatly. "My jerky brothers would bug us the entire time." Rocky put her hands on her hips and looked each girl straight in the eye. "Now, are we going to help Annie out and be real Cupids?" she barked. "Or should we change our name to the Scaredy Cats and forget the whole thing?"

Gwen looked up at the wooden fort and shrugged. "OK, I'll go up there. But if that ladder breaks, and I fall and break all the bones in my body, I'm never giving you another Twinkie as long as I live."

McGee went up first, while Rocky stayed at the bottom in case anybody had any trouble. McGee scrambled up the wooden ladder until she reached the bottom of the fort. A piece of wood served as a trapdoor and she flipped it open and stuck her head inside. "Hey, this is pretty neat."

"I told you," Rocky said, giving Gwen an extra shove in the bottom.

"Don't push," Gwen grumbled. "I'm going as fast as I can."

One by one the girls clambered into the fort. Once they were all inside, Rocky shut the door and bolted it. She pulled some blankets out of the corner and tossed them to the others.

"It's not as cold as I thought it would be," Mary Bubnik said. "This is really cozy."

Rocky smiled, looking very pleased. "Thanks. I built it myself."

"Really?" McGee said, impressed.

"With a little help from my dad."

Zan dug into her totebag and pulled out her lavender notepad. "I think we should officially call this meeting of the Cupids to order."

"About time, too," Rocky said, shaking her head. "I thought we'd never get any privacy."

"Should we do our secret sign, to sort of start things off?" Mary Bubnik asked, placing her hands across her heart.

"Good idea," McGee said, following suit. The others did likewise and McGee announced in a low voice, "This meeting of the Cupids is officially begun." She nodded at Zan and said, "Let's get right down to business."

Zan opened her notepad and laid it flat on her

lap. "Our purpose today is to come up with a plan for Operation Annie," she said. "Our goal is to find her a boyfriend by Valentine's Day."

"That's only a week and a half away," Gwen said. "How will we ever do it?"

Mary Bubnik raised her hand. "I think we should talk to all of the boys at the academy, and see if any of them would be right for Annie."

"What if none of them are?" Gwen asked.

"Then we have to investigate all of the available bachelors in the area of the academy," Zan replied.

"You mean, like in stores?" Mary Bubnik asked.

Zan nodded. "And in offices and restaurants."

"Why just that area?" McGee asked.

"Well, she spends most of her life at the ballet studio," Gwen reasoned. "They would have to work near there, so they can see her."

Rocky shrugged. "That makes sense."

"There is one other possibility," Zan said slowly. "But we should use it *only* as a last resort."

"What's that?" Rocky demanded.

"The Personals."

"The Personals?" Mary Bubnik looked perplexed. "What are those?"

"Well, they're like the want ads," Gwen explained. "Only these are for people."

"You mean, people advertise for a date?" Mary Bubnik gasped. "That's incredible! What do they say?"

"Here, I'll read one for you." Zan unfolded a piece of newspaper that she had hidden in the zipper compartment of her purse. She cleared her throat and carefully read, " 'Romantic, caring, and handsome male seeks down-to-earth lady with a sense of humor. Would like you to enjoy sunrises, sunsets, picnics, music, dancing, and life.' "

"Make me gag!" McGee giggled. "That's so corny."

Zan looked at her indignantly. "I think it's sweet."

"Give me that," Gwen said, snatching the newspaper clipping out of Zan's hands. "Oooh, how about this one? 'Short, not tall, cute, not ugly, large, not fat, female looking for a nice guy who likes the beach, spiced shrimp, and quiet nights at home.' "

"In other words," Rocky cracked, "a dull, not fun, nerdy, not cool, geek."

Gwen stuck her tongue out at Rocky. McGee, who'd been reading the page over Gwen's back, said, "How about this? 'Handsome, lonely male, into bodybuilding, likes hiking, boating, skating, and skiing and seeks female liking same.' "

"Why should he be lonely?" Gwen wondered sourly. "He sounds like he's always looking at his muscles in the mirror."

"I don't know, y'all," Mary Bubnik said. "I think these are all kind of weird."

"Well, I do, too," Zan agreed. "That's why we only use them as a last resort."

The others nodded in agreement. "So, what do we have?" Rocky asked.

"A three-point plan," Zan said, holding up her notepad. "On Saturday we meet early before class and interview the boys at the studio."

"Gosh, what do we say to them?" Mary Bubnik asked.

There was a long pause.

"I don't know," McGee admitted. "I guess you'd ask them questions like, do you have a girlfriend?"

"That's good," Zan nodded. "That's real important."

"No kidding," Rocky agreed. "We can eliminate 'em right off with that one."

"What are your hobbies?" Gwen suggested.

"Do you like Annie?" Mary said.

"But that's only good for boys who already know Annie," Zan corrected.

"Oh, right!"

Zan looked up from her notepad and said, "This is a good start but we'll need more."

"I think we should each go home and think up some important questions," McGee said, "then bring them in on Saturday. That way we'll be completely prepared."

"Good deal." Rocky looked around at the others and said, "I think that takes care of business for Operation Annie, don't you?"

"It'd better," Gwen said with a shiver. "I'm getting cold."

"Let's do the secret sign," McGee instructed, "and then we'll adjourn to the house."

They solemnly crossed their hearts, then began folding up the blankets.

"I can't wait for Saturday," Mary Bubnik giggled. "Do you think Zach will be back?"

"After the way all of you acted?" Rocky snorted with disgust. "Not a chance."

"What do you mean, how *we* acted?" McGee demanded.

"Well, you practically drooled all over him."

Her remark was greeted by a chorus of protests. Suddenly the tree began to shake violently.

"What's happening?" Mary Bubnik screamed, clutching at Zan.

"It's an earthquake!" Gwen squealed.

"The fort is going to collapse!" Zan cried.

"Relax," Rocky said calmly. "It's just my stupid brothers, shaking the tree."

She pointed down through the trapdoor. Joey, David, and Michael were clustered at the bottom, grinning fiendishly up at the girls, while they tugged and pulled at the tree trunk.

"Stop that right now, you creeps!" Rocky screamed. "Or you're going to get it."

They mimicked her voice, and she got even madder.

53

"I'm telling Mom," she warned. "I mean it."

McGee tugged her by the sleeve and whispered, "Don't get mad, Rocky. Get even."

"How?"

McGee tore off a piece of notepaper and chewed it carefully, then wadded it up into a tight little ball. "We'll nail 'em with spitwads."

"Oooh, gross," Gwen said, making a face.

"Yeah, well, now's not the time to get squeamish," McGee said. She tore off four little squares and handed them around. They chewed methodically as the tree wobbled back and forth. Then McGee shouted, "OK, Cupids, let 'em have it!"

They leaned over the side and showered the hapless boys with wet missiles. The boys raised their arms over their heads to protect themselves from the onslaught of soggy paper.

Rocky hit Joey right in the forehead with her spitwad. "Yuck!" he shouted and ran off toward the house, wiping off his face. David and Michael followed close behind.

"Bull's-eye!" Rocky raised her arms over her head in victory.

McGee gave Rocky a high five and shouted, "Score one for the Cupids!"

Chapter Six

"I can't believe Zach didn't show up today!" Gwen complained that Saturday as the gang trooped out of class. The dressing room was like a morgue. Even the Bunheads, who were normally chatty, changed their clothes in stunned silence.

"How could he do that to us?" Zan moaned. She and practically every other girl in the class had spent the week looking forward to seeing him again.

"I dieted for three days," Gwen said, "all for nothing."

Mary Bubnik nodded. "I even practiced the skating steps, just in case Annie paired us up again."

Gwen stepped behind the full-length mirror to

change her clothes. "I feel like eating a whole pack of Twinkies right now, just to show him."

"I'm not surprised he didn't show up today," Rocky said, slipping her jeans on over her leotard. "You guys scared him off."

"How?" McGee challenged.

"By falling all over him in class last week."

"At least we were friendly," Gwen shouted from behind the mirror.

"Yeah," McGee said, pulling a sweatshirt over her head. "I'll bet he didn't come back 'cause you scared him."

"Now, how could I scare him?" Rocky asked. "I didn't even talk to him."

"You made fun of him by calling him Zachary-Thackary," Zan pointed out.

Gwen took a big bite out of a Snickers bar. "And you laughed at him when he and Trisha danced across the floor."

Rocky put her hands on her hips. "Well, he must be a real wimp if he can't take a joke."

She threw back the curtain and stepped into the lobby just as the class in Studio A was letting out. Several of the male dancers from the ballet company appeared. They had towels draped around their necks and their faces were gleaming with sweat.

"Look, you guys!" Mary Bubnik gasped. "It's Zach!"

He was speaking to Mr. Anton, the director of the

56

academy, just inside the studio door. As he stepped into the lobby, Mary Bubnik shouted, "Hi, Zach! We sure missed you in class today."

"What's the matter?" Rocky taunted. "Was our class too hard for you?"

"No." Zach smiled, revealing the dimple in his cheek. "Mr. Anton scheduled a technique class for the guys and asked me if I wanted to take it."

"Does that mean you won't be in our group anymore?" Gwen asked, trying to swallow her mouthful of candy bar, and vowing never to eat another one as long as she lived.

Zach shook his head. "Today was a special deal. I'll be back in class next week."

"Just in time for the Valentine's Day party," Mary Bubnik hinted.

"Oh, that's right," Zach said. "I forgot all about it."

"Well, I haven't." Mary giggled. "I've already got my valentines done. I've got one for every single person in our class." Just to make sure he'd gotten the point, she batted her eyelashes at him.

"Make me gag," Rocky muttered under her breath.

Zach started backing away toward the men's dressing room. "Yeah, well, I guess I'll see you next week." As he turned to leave, Rocky stuck her foot out. Zach tripped over it and nearly crashed into the wall.

"Watch it, twinkle toes!" Rocky chuckled.

Zach shot her a bewildered look as he disappeared into the men's dressing room.

"What were you trying to do?" McGee hissed. "Break his leg?"

"Hey, back off!" Rocky said. "That was just a joke."

"Some joke," Gwen muttered. "Now Zach is going to hate all of us."

"Well, at least I wasn't drooling all over him."

"Who was drooling?" Gwen demanded.

"You" — Rocky reached out and wiped a smudge of chocolate off Gwen's cheek — "and here's the evidence."

"Oh, no!" Gwen's hands flew to her face. "Was that there the whole time we were talking to him?"

Nobody answered. Gwen groaned and threw herself on the couch. "How humiliating! I'll never be able to face him again."

Zan, who had kept very quiet for most of the discussion, suddenly spoke up. "Do you realize this is a perfect time to do Plan One of — " She crossed her hands over her heart and whispered, "Operation Annie?"

Gwen sat up on the couch. "What do you mean?"

"At this moment, all of the possible candidates for Annie's valentine are in that room," Zan pointed at the men's dressing room.

"What do you want us to do?" Rocky demanded.

"Barge into a roomful of guys in their underwear and start asking questions?"

"Of course not," Zan blushed. "We can knock very politely and ask to speak to one of them."

"No way." Rocky shook her head. "I'm not knocking on that door."

"What are you, chicken?" McGee asked.

Rocky's eye twitched. Nobody called her "chicken" and got away with it. "Of course not!"

"I *dare* you to knock on that dressing room and ask the first guy who answers some questions." McGee stared Rocky straight in the eye and grinned smugly. "I don't think you can do it."

"Piece of cake," Rocky said, trying to sound casual. "Watch this."

"Look!" Mary Bubnik pointed to a tall, muscular boy stepping through the curtain into the hallway. "Isn't that Derek McClellan?" Derek McClellan was the leading male dancer for the Deerfield Ballet and incredibly handsome.

"It sure is," Gwen said. She turned and smiled at Rocky. "Go ahead, Miss Cool."

Rocky gave her a withering look, then strolled casually over to the boy.

"Yo, Derek!" she called, waving one hand. "Talk to you a minute?"

Derek looked over to her in surprise. "What do you need?"

"Thirty seconds of your time." Rocky tried to keep her voice cool and confident but inside she felt a little shaky.

He checked his watch, and shrugged. "OK, but make it snappy."

"I'm doing an article for my school paper about the leading dancers for the ballet company," Rocky began.

"Oh?" He raised one eyebrow.

"A lot of the girls in my school want to know" — she ticked off the questions on her fingers — "are you single, do you have a girlfriend, and do you like to date?"

"That's kind of personal, isn't it?" Derek said coldly. "What's that got to do with ballet?"

Rocky could feel her face get red at his rebuff. She tried to make a joke of it. "Well, you know how girls are. They already know how great a dancer you are. They'd just like to know a bit more about your private life. For Valentine's Day."

"I don't think that's any of your business," Derek said. He checked his watch. "Your thirty seconds are up, and I have to go."

He started to step around her when Rocky grabbed the strap on his bag in desperation. "Uh, how about your friends? I mean, do you think any of them would be interested in being featured in my school newspaper?"

For the first time a smile appeared on Derek's

face. "I don't know. Why don't you ask them your-self?"

Before she could say a word, he whipped the curtain to the men's dressing room open wide. Rocky squeezed her eyes shut and covered her face.

"Don't look!" Mary Bubnik squealed.

There was dead silence, followed by deep laugh-ter. Rocky peeked between her fingers and saw the reason why. All of the guys were standing in a semi-circle, completely dressed, with wide grins on their faces.

Rocky dropped her hands. "Ha. Ha. Very funny."

This made the boys laugh even harder, and she completely lost her nerve. It was Gwen who came to her rescue.

"Listen, would any one of you guys care to be included in our Valentine's Day raffle?" Gwen asked, stepping forward to the edge of the door. "All you have to do is answer two questions."

The boys looked at each other, then shouted, "No!"

Their voices were so strong that the girls auto-matically stepped backward. This made the boys chuckle even louder as they moved past the gang through the lobby and out of the Academy.

Rocky hung her head, totally humiliated. "Boy, did I blow it."

McGee suddenly felt bad for her friend. "Listen, you gave it your best shot."

61

Zan patted Rocky on the shoulder. "If it makes you feel any better, I don't think any of them were right for Annie."

"Especially Derek McClellan," Gwen said. "I think he's kind of a snob."

Mary Bubnik nodded. "Annie needs someone much nicer."

"Did anyone notice if Zach was laughing at me?" Rocky dug the toe of her tennis shoe into the floor.

"What difference does it make?" Gwen asked. "I thought you said he was just a dumb boy."

Rocky threw her head back defiantly. "He is. I just thought if he laughed at me, I'd threaten to break his arm."

Zan gasped. "Don't you dare. You may not like him, but we do."

The others nodded vigorously and Rocky shrugged. "Maybe I'll give him one more chance."

"Good." Zan smiled at her and then got back to business. "Have we questioned all the bachelors in this building?"

"Not quite," Mary Bubnik pointed out. "There's still Mr. Anton and Ralph the janitor."

"Mr. Anton is *ages* older than Annie," Gwen said. "Besides, I think he's kind of strict." She added logically, "I guess you'd have to be to run an entire ballet academy."

"And Ralph is married," Zan said.

"How do you know that?" Mary asked.

"His kids go to my school," Zan replied. "Or at least some of them do. He has seven children."

McGee blew her bangs off her forehead in frustration. "Well, it looks like Plan One is a bust."

"What do we do now?" Mary Bubnik asked.

"What do we do?" Zan flipped to the next page of her lavender pad. "It's time for Plan Two."

Chapter
Seven

"We have to talk to perfect strangers?" Mary Bubnik asked as the five girls stood on the street in front of Hillberry Hall.

"Of course," McGee replied. "How else are we going to find Mr. Right?"

"My mother told me never to do that," Mary Bubnik said hesitantly.

"That's when they try to talk to *you*," Gwen explained. "This is different. *We're* talking to *them*."

"Besides, what could happen?" Rocky added. "They'll be outnumbered. There's five of us to one of them." She aimed a karate kick at the streetlight. "Any funny stuff, they'll never know what hit 'em."

"Listen, I think we should start over there," Gwen

declared, pointing to the Polar Bear Ice Cream store on the corner. "The guy who runs it is kind of cute, and just think — Annie could have all the free ice cream she wants."

"Ballerinas don't eat ice cream," Rocky said. "Remember? They're always on diets."

Zan pointed in the opposite direction. "I think the medical building is the place to look. Doctors are terribly rich and could take Annie to all sorts of wonderful places."

Rocky jogged down the street ahead of them. "Come on, you guys," she urged, "we have to hurry. My brother Jay is picking me up in a few minutes."

The girls quickened their pace and moments later were standing in front of the small brick building. Zan looked nervously at Rocky. "What do we do now?"

"We go inside," Rocky instructed.

Zan and Mary Bubnik gulped.

"Then we stroll casually past the offices until we find the right doctor who'll be Annie's valentine."

"Oh, good, we have several to choose from." McGee pointed to the brass plate on the side of the building. "Dr. Wilson, Dr. Cunningham, Dr. De-Santis, and Dr. Ott."

Rocky pulled back the big oak door and held it open for the others. They filed past her one by one into the foyer. The reception room consisted of several leather couches grouped around shiny coffee tables littered with magazines. A lady dressed in white with a nurse's cap perched on her head sat inside a glassed-in office that stretched across one side of the room. She was busy answering the phone and didn't see them come in.

Rocky let the heavy door swing shut behind her, and the sudden noise made Mary Bubnik shriek with fright.

"What are you trying to do," Gwen hissed, "blow the whole operation?"

"Guess I'm a little nervous," Mary said with a giggle.

"Just stick close," Rocky whispered, "and follow me."

The gang moved in a tight clump toward a hall with a sign above it that read Offices. Rocky waited until the nurse in the glassed-in booth turned her back to reach for a file before leading the girls down the carpeted hall.

Dr. Ott's office door was slightly ajar and they peeked inside. A short, bald man with glasses was sitting at a desk, working on some papers.

"Too old," Mary Bubnik whispered. The others nodded and moved on.

Dr. Wilson was just going into his office. He was tall and gangly, with big ears that stuck out on either side of his head. "Too weird," Rocky judged.

They rounded the corner and spotted another man in a white doctor's coat, who stood in the corridor consulting with another nurse. He had a friendly face but his big, round stomach stuck out over his pants.

"Too short," Zan said. "And fat."

"What's wrong with fat?" Gwen hissed.

"It's just not right for Annie," McGee explained. "She's an athlete, remember?" She gestured for them to back up.

They did and stopped in front of the door that read *Dr. DeSantis.* "He's our last hope," Rocky whispered.

They were just about to knock on the door when suddenly it opened. A nice-looking young man in a plaid shirt and a blue tie peered out at them. "Yes, may I help you?"

"We're looking for Doctor DeSantis," Mary Bubnik answered.

"You've found him." The dark-haired man smiled down at them.

"Are you sure?" Gwen squinted at him suspiciously. "Where's your doctor's coat?"

McGee jabbed Gwen in the side and hissed, "Not all doctors wear white coats."

"Every doctor I've ever seen has worn one," Gwen shot back. "A white coat *and* a stethoscope."

The girls eyed him warily. He was wearing tan corduroy pants and brown loafers. Maybe Gwen was right. Maybe he *was* just a patient pretending to be a doctor.

67

"He doesn't even have a name tag," Gwen said, pointing at his empty chest accusingly. "All *real* doctors have name tags."

"Now, hold on a minute," the man protested. "I have all of those things in my office. See?" He held open the door and the five girls peeked inside. "My white coat is on my chair. My stethoscope is in the pocket of my coat."

"What about your name tag?" Gwen demanded.

"Right there on the desk," the man replied. "It's broken."

"Oh." Gwen felt too embarrassed to even look at him.

"*Now* do you believe I'm a doctor?" Dr. DeSantis asked.

"Yes, she does." Zan grabbed Gwen's arm and tugged her down the hall. "We're terribly sorry to have bothered you."

"Wait a minute!" Dr. DeSantis called after them. "Is that all you wanted to know — if I'm a real doctor?"

"Well actually, we do have one more question," Gwen said, locking her knees.

"Yes?" The doctor smiled.

"Are you married?"

Dr. DeSantis looked surprised for only a second. Then he answered, "No, I'm not."

"Great!" Rocky said, clapping her hands together. "Thanks, Doc!"

McGee pointed toward the nearest exit. "Come on, everybody."

Gwen stood her ground. "We can't leave yet. I have some more questions."

"Oh, no, you don't." Rocky and McGee got behind her and pushed her down the hall to the green Exit sign. Once they were outside McGee barked, "Who do you think you are — Perry Mason, attorney-at-law?"

"Yeah," Rocky said. "What's the idea, giving him the third degree? Do you want to blow everything?"

"It never hurts to be cautious," Gwen said wisely.

"I like him," Mary Bubnik giggled. "I think he and Annie will really hit it off."

"I do, too," Zan chimed in.

Rocky put one finger to her chin. "Now all we have to do is figure out a way for Annie to meet him today."

"Today?" Gwen repeated. "Why does it have to be today?" She looked longingly at the sign above Hi Lo's restaurant. "I'm hungry."

"Because they have to have time to meet and fall in love so he can get her a wonderful gift for Valentine's Day," Zan explained.

"Which is exactly one week away," McGee pointed out.

"OK, OK," Gwen said reluctantly. "But how do we get Annie out of the studio to meet Dr. DeSantis?"

"We don't have to worry about that," Mary Bubnik

69

replied. "She's already outside, and walking this way."

"What?" The girls looked down the street at Hillberry Hall. Annie, dressed in a long black wool coat and muffler, was making her way down the white marble steps in front of the building.

"Faint!" Rocky hissed suddenly.

"Huh?" Gwen blinked at her.

"I said, faint. Right now!"

Four girls dropped to the sidewalk.

"Not everybody," Rocky said, rolling her eyes. "Just one of you."

The four girls leaped to their feet, looking at each other confusedly. Annie was already near the bottom of the steps. "Oh, brother!" Rocky muttered and keeled over onto the icy sidewalk.

"Annie!" McGee shouted, finally realizing what Rocky was up to. "Please, help us. Rocky's fainted."

The other girls took up the cry. "Annie, help! She's fainted. Oh, no! What are we going to do?" Gwen wrung her hands convincingly while Zan buried her face in her handkerchief and pretended to cry.

Rocky cracked one eye open slightly. "Don't overdo it," she muttered out of the corner of her mouth. "I haven't died, I've just fainted."

Annie heard their cries and was kneeling by Rocky's side in a flash. "What happened, girls?"

"We were just standing here, waiting for the bus," McGee explained, adding a little catch to her voice, "when Rocky just fell to the ground."

70

"Maybe she overdid it in dance class today," Gwen added.

"Oh, no, do you think so?" Annie felt Rocky's forehead with her palm, then lifted one of the girl's hands. Rocky was completely limp.

"Maybe you should get a doctor," Zan suggested softly. She pointed to the oak door directly behind them and added, "In there."

"Yes, good idea," Annie stood up, definitely flustered. "Maybe he's got some smelling salts."

"Right through there." Gwen took Annie by the arm and led her toward the brick building. "But don't ask for Dr. Ott."

"Or Dr. Wilson," Mary shouted.

"Ask for Dr. DeSantis," McGee said. "We hear he's the best."

Gwen nodded. "An expert on fainting."

"Hey, what's going on here?" a male voice suddenly called from behind them.

Rocky cracked open one eye and groaned under her breath. "Oh, no! It's my brother Jay."

Gwen, who was still trying to shove Annie into the doctor's office, called back, "Rocky fainted, but don't worry, Annie is going to get Dr. DeSantis."

"Hold on a second," Jay ordered as he knelt down by his sister. "It's all right," he called to Annie. "I'm Jay Garcia, Rocky's brother."

"I'm Annie Springer, Rocky's ballet teacher."

"Nice to meet you."

71

"The girls think we should get a doctor," Annie said.

"A doctor?" Jay looked down at Rocky, then up at the other four. "What for? This kid's never been sick a day in her life."

"There's always a first time," Gwen said reasonably.

"Come on, Rocky, wake up." He patted her cheeks with his hands. "It's me, Jay."

Rocky moaned a little, just to let him know she didn't like being hit in the face.

"Look," Jay said, "she's coming around."

"Just to be on the safe side," Annie said, "I think we should take her to a doctor." She gestured toward the building behind her.

Jay scooped her up in his arms and Rocky had to think fast. If her brother went into the doctor's office with Annie, Dr. DeSantis might think they were going together and the whole scheme would be ruined. There was no way out of it. She had to make a miraculous recovery on the spot.

"Jay, what are you doing?" Rocky cried out, opening her eyes wide. "Put me down this minute."

"Hey, calm down, Rocky," he said. "You fainted. Annie thinks you should see a doctor."

"I don't need a doctor," Rocky said. "What I need is — um, *food.* Yeah, that's it, I think I must have gotten weak from dieting."

"Why would you be dieting?" Jay demanded, still

holding her firmly in his arms. "You're already skinny."

"For dance class," Rocky replied, smiling sweetly at Annie. "All the best dancers are extra thin."

"Oh, Rocky!" Annie came over and patted her gently on the arm. "Dancers do try to watch their weight, but they don't starve themselves. What did you have to eat today?"

"Some Wheat Thins and a cup of soup." Rocky groaned a little to make it sound like she was in pain.

Annie shook her head. "What you need is some good, solid food."

Gwen's face brightened at the mention of food. "How about Hi Lo's? He could make her some noodles, and the rest of us ice cream sundaes."

Annie looked up at Rocky's brother. "How does that sound to you?"

"OK by me." Jay smiled warmly at Annie. Rocky recognized his lopsided grin as the one her brother had used to melt the hearts of all the girls when he was in high school on base.

"Put me down," she growled to her brother. As soon as he set her back on her feet, she stomped across the street to Hi Lo's. She flung open the big glass door and marched straight to the one and only booth in the back of the tiny restaurant. McGee and the gang hurried to join her. They crowded in beside her, while Jay and Annie sat down at the counter.

"Just take it easy, Rocky," her brother called. "We'll get you some food in a jiffy."

"You'll be fine," Annie added.

Mr. Lo came out of the back and they explained what had happened. He glanced over in surprise when Annie told him Rocky had fainted. "Leave it to me," he said, hurrying back into the kitchen.

"Well, Jay completely ruined Plan Two," Rocky said, slumping against the back of the booth. "Sorry, gang."

"Maybe we could come back on Monday and try the same thing again," Mary Bubnik suggested.

Zan shook her head. "Dr. DeSantis may not work on Mondays."

"Besides," Rocky added, "I can't faint twice."

"Maybe on Monday you could pretend to be hit by a car," McGee said hopefully. "That's pretty easy to fake. You just hit a passing car on the trunk with your hand, then drop to the ground."

"But then you'd have to deal with the driver," Gwen pointed out logically. "What if he gets upset and calls an ambulance or the police?"

"I could be arrested for faking an accident," Rocky moaned. "No thanks!"

"Rocky's right," Zan said. "I think we should consider Plan Two a failure."

"So now what do we do?" Mary Bubnik drawled.

Zan took a deep breath and whispered, "I think it's time to move to Plan Three."

"But we were only going to use that as a last resort," Gwen said, wide-eyed.

Zan shrugged. "Time is running out. Either we do something about Operation" — she gestured toward Annie at the counter — "you-know-who *today,* or we quit."

"Never!" Rocky and McGee chorused.

"So it's Plan Three," Gwen whispered.

Zan pulled a piece of paper out of her purse and placed it on the table in front of them. Three lines of writing were typed neatly upon it.

"Then here it is," she announced. "Our ad for the Personals."

As Zan picked it up to read it aloud, Gwen muttered darkly, "I hope we know what we're getting into."

Chapter Eight

Rocky convinced her brother that she had left her hat back at the dance studio. Then she and the gang hurried out of Hi Lo's, calling, "We'll be back as soon as we find it!"

A few minutes later, the five friends stood in front of the imposing offices of the *Deerfield Times*. They were in an old stone building with a metal sculpture of the planet Earth perched on the roof. As the globe spun, words appeared on its face, telling the time and date and the headline from the newspaper that day.

The girls pushed through the revolving door that spun them into the marble-tiled lobby. To their right a bank of elevators opened and shut with a constant dinging of bells, whisking people up to the various floors.

"Where's the newspaper?" Mary Bubnik asked, looking around uncertainly.

"Over here, guys," Rocky called from beside the elevators. A metal directory hung on the wall listing the various occupants of the building and what floor they were on. "The *Deerfield Times,*" Rocky read out loud. "Floors three through ten."

A bell rang and the elevator doors opened up. They jumped inside and Gwen pushed one of the buttons. "We'll start on the third floor."

When the doors opened again, the girls found themselves facing a huge open room lined with dozens of desks. Some people were banging away at their typewriters, others were running up and down the aisles waving pieces of paper, and they all seemed to be talking at once.

"There must be a hundred people in there," McGee gasped.

"Well, what did you expect?" Gwen asked. "This is a newspaper. They've got reporters, and typesetters, and secretaries, and editors — "

"And paper boys," Mary Bubnik added.

"I guess I didn't think it would be this big," McGee said. "It's kind of scary."

The others nodded in agreement. With all these

people bustling around them, the girls suddenly felt like they were back in the first grade again, not knowing where anything was.

"Somebody ask where the Personals Department is," Rocky urged.

"Not me!" Gwen said, backing away into the elevator.

Mary Bubnik was right beside her. "Me, neither. They'll throw us out of here."

"I think Zan should ask," McGee said.

"Why me?" Zan exclaimed, a horrified look on her face. "I'm the biggest chicken of all of us."

"But you're the tallest," McGee replied. "They'll take you more seriously, because they'll think you're older."

"McGee's right." Rocky pointed to a surly-looking man with a cigar, who was standing by the water fountain reading a newspaper. "Go ask him."

When Zan hesitated, Gwen crossed her hands over her heart. "Remember, it's for Annie."

Zan forced herself to walk stiffly over to the man with the cigar. "Excuse me, sir," she began. "Could you tell me where people place ads?"

"What?" he barked, cupping one hand behind his ear. "Speak up, kid, I can't hear you."

Zan took a deep breath. "Could you please tell me where I might place a personal ad?"

"Personals?" he replied, blowing a huge cloud of smoke from his cigar. "That'd be Sophie Washburn." He jerked his thumb toward the back of the room. "Go on back. You can't miss her, she's wearing that awful dress of hers again."

"Thank you," Zan said politely. The man grunted and turned back to his paper. Zan gestured for the others to follow, and they quickly wove their way through the maze of desks toward the back of the room.

Sophie Washburn wasn't hard to find. In fact, she would have been hard to miss. She was a large, rather plump woman, with huge earrings that bounced and jangled noisily whenever she turned her head. Her hair was dyed black and done up in a beehive-shaped hairdo that didn't move because it was sealed with hairspray. Her dark red fingernail polish matched her lipstick perfectly.

But what made Sophie Washburn recognizable from any distance was the bright pink and lime-green flowered dress she wore. It lit up the drab office like a lighthouse in the fog.

When the girls arrived at her desk, Sophie had her phone cradled on her shoulder and was busy scribbling a message down with one hand while she sipped a steaming cup of coffee with the other.

"Be with you girls in just a second," she said, flashing a warm, toothy smile at them.

"At least she's nice," Mary Bubnik whispered gratefully into Zan's ear.

Sophie set the phone back on its cradle with a

79

crash and said, "So. What can I do for you ladies?"

Suddenly Zan's eyes widened and she exclaimed, "You're 'Dear Sophie,' aren't you?"

"Why, yes, I am." A pleased smile curled the edges of Sophie's mouth. "How nice of you to notice!"

"I recognized you from your picture," Zan said. "I read your column faithfully."

"Me, too," Mary Bubnik chimed in. "Right after the comics, and my horoscope."

"Well, that's very flattering." She gestured to the girls to come closer. "Pull up a chair. Make yourselves at home."

The girls looked around and discovered there was not a chair in sight.

"Howie!" Sophie shouted at the top of her lungs. "Bring me five chairs, will ya? I've got some important fans over here who need to sit down."

Quick as a wink, a fellow in overalls hurried over with several folding chairs. Soon Zan and the girls were sitting comfortably in a half-circle in front of Sophie's desk.

"There!" she said, folding her hands in front of her. Each finger had a ring of a different style and shape. "That's much better. Now, tell me what you need to know."

"We want to place an ad in the Personals, and we're not sure how to go about it." Zan smiled and added, "We were kind of wondering if you could help us."

"I'd be delighted!" Sophie exclaimed. "You girls caught me at the right time." Sophie took a sip of her coffee, and one last bite of a chocolate-covered doughnut that had been sitting in front of her. With her mouth full she mumbled, "I just *this minute* finished my 'Dear Sophie' column for tomorrow's paper."

"Did you get some good letters this week?" Zan asked eagerly.

"You better believe it, honey."

"Can you tell us about them?" Mary Bubnik asked, with a mischievous giggle.

"Well, I really shouldn't. . . ." Sophie put one long, painted fingernail up to her lips and thought for a moment. "But, since you girls are such big fans, a little preview wouldn't hurt." Sophie looked over both shoulders and gestured for the girls to lean forward. "The first letter" she whispered, "is signed, 'Desperate in Danville.' "

"What are they desperate about?" Gwen asked.

"Well, it seems that Desperate's husband divorced her and ran off with her very best friend."

"That rat!" Rocky declared.

Sophie nodded. "I couldn't have said it better myself, hon. But that's not the worst of it. As soon as he married her best friend, he decided he wanted to date Desperate again!"

"Did she date him?" McGee asked.

"Of course. That's what makes her so desperate."

Sophie leaned forward. "Now he wants to divorce her best friend and marry Desperate again!"

The air was filled with cries of outrage from the gang. Then Zan asked, "What did you tell her to do?"

Sophie held up her hands and sat back in her chair. "I *never* reveal my answers early." She paused, then said, "Let's just say I told her that if she goes back with that bum, she should have her head examined."

"I agree," Zan said.

"Me, too!" McGee echoed. The girls clapped their hands, and Sophie bowed her head slightly to acknowledge their applause.

"But enough about me," she said, waving her hand in the air with a loud clanking of her copper bracelets. "Let's talk about your ad. May I ask which of you girls this is for?"

"It's not for us," they chorused. "It's for a friend."

"Of about your age?" Sophie asked, tilting her head to look at them.

"Oh, no," Zan said, digging in her purse for the ad she'd written. "Our friend is much older than us."

"Maybe nineteen," Gwen added.

"Ah, a mature woman of the world," Sophie said.

"And she's a dancer," McGee said proudly.

"Good, good." Sophie took another sip of coffee. "Dancers always get lots of responses."

82

"Here's what I wrote." Zan sheepishly handed her the slip of paper. "I know it needs some work but —"

Sophie held up one hand and interrupted Zan with another loud clink of bracelets. "Don't apologize. Just let me read it, and we'll see what we can do." She cleared her throat noisily and read the ad out loud. "Pretty ballerina looking for valentine with a heart of gold. Must be young and handsome."

Sophie set the paper down on her desk, and the girls waited anxiously for her response. She pursed her lips thoughtfully, then said, "It's got a good start but —"

"But what?" Rocky said. "Is something wrong?"

"Oh, no!" Sophie reassured her. "It just needs a little. . . ." She searched for the right word. "Fixing up, that's all."

"I really like the heart of gold part," Mary Bubnik said, "but don't you think Annie is more than just pretty? I'd say she's beautiful."

Zan nodded. "You're absolutely right." She took out her pen and carefully drew a line through the word "pretty" and wrote "beautiful" in the space above it.

"Beautiful. Now *that's* a good word." Sophie nodded her approval. "OK, now tell me, what color are her eyes?"

"Blue," Gwen answered immediately.

Sophie shook her head. "In one of these ads, you never just say blue. You want to say what *kind* of blue — navy, royal, sapphire, aqua — "

"Sky-blue!" Mary Bubnik exclaimed.

"Good! Write that down." Sophie pointed at the paper. "Now I think you're getting the hang of it."

"I think we should say that she's looking for some-one who's in good shape," McGee added. "After all, Annie is a dancer."

"That's right, honey." Sophie bobbed her head up and down and her earrings jangled. "She wouldn't want some slob for a date. You better say, 'handsome, well-muscled, young athlete.'"

Zan carefully printed that phrase over the top of her advertisement.

"And I think he should be adventurous," Rocky chimed in. "We want him to take her to fun and unusual places."

"Like great restaurants," Gwen said.

"That's using your noggin'." Sophie patted Gwen on the head. "You see, it's all in how you say it. If you write, 'likes good food,' she might wind up with some ding-a-ling who thinks a bowl of chili is real cooking, y'know what I'm sayin'? You need to use the word *gourmet* in your ad." She gestured to Zan and said, "Write this down. 'Enjoys gourmet dinners by candlelight.'"

Mary Bubnik giggled. "That sounds *so* romantic!"

"Romance is my middle name," Sophie declared, patting her bouffant hairdo. "Sophie 'Romance' Washburn."

Meanwhile, Zan, who had been writing furiously, put down her pen and held up her finished ad. "OK, everybody, how does this sound? 'Beautiful ballerina, with sky-blue eyes, seeks handsome, well-muscled young athlete, who enjoys gourmet dinners by candlelight, adventure, and good books. If you are a valentine with a heart of gold, send your picture and a letter to me, care of the *Deerfield Times.*'"

Zan set the paper down on her lap, and the girls looked to Sophie for her reaction. Sophie took a sip of her coffee, rolled it around in her mouth, and then set the cup back down. "I like it," she declared.

"Yea!" The girls couldn't help jumping out of their chairs and cheering.

"It has everything," Sophie continued. "Romance, excitement, and even a little mystery." She folded her hands in front of her. "You should get a lot of responses, I guarantee it."

"By when?" Mary Bubnik asked. "Tomorrow?"

"Good heavens, no!" Sophie replied. "First all of the eligible bachelors have to read the ad, then they have to get a picture of themselves, and *then* write a response and mail it or drop it by the desk here."

"How long will that take?" Gwen asked dejectedly.

"Let me see." Sophie flipped open her desk calendar. Each page was packed with little slips of paper with notes to herself. "I'd say, by Wednesday afternoon."

"Great!" Rocky clapped her hands together. "That will give us two days to pick the perfect valentine for Annie."

"Trust me," Sophie replied with a wink. She slipped their paper into a manila folder and said, "Now, who's paying for this?"

It only cost a few dollars for a week's worth of advertising. The girls rummaged through their purses and quickly came up with the right amount. Then McGee looked up at a clock hanging from the wall and shouted, "Geez Louise! We've been gone for over half an hour."

"Yeah," Rocky agreed, pulling her hat out of her pocket. "My brother's going to be real miffed if I don't get back to Hi's right away."

Zan reached out and shook Sophie's hand enthusiastically. "Thank you so much for all your help. We'll never forget it."

"Believe me, the pleasure's all mine," Sophie said.

The girls started to leave when Gwen suddenly stopped. "Wait a minute. I have to ask Sophie one more question."

"Not again," McGee groaned.

Gwen ignored McGee's comment. "Sophie?"

"Yes, dear?"

"What advice would you give to five girls who like the same boy?"

"Four girls," Rocky corrected.

Gwen rolled her eyes. "OK, *four* girls."

Sophie put one long painted fingernail to her lips. "That's a tough one. All's fair in love and war, is one way people look at this sort of thing. But if you want my opinion —"

The girls clustered tightly around Sophie's desk, waiting for her words of wisdom.

"If your friendship means a lot to you —"

The girls looked at each other and nodded solemnly.

"Then forget the boy. Keep your friends — they last longer."

That wasn't really what the girls wanted to hear, but they thanked Sophie anyway.

"Think nothing of it," Sophie replied modestly. The phone rang again, and as she raised it to her ear and lifted her mug to her lips, she shouted, "Come back and see me sometime, will ya?"

"You can count on it!" McGee called.

The girls flew down the street to Hi Lo's restaurant, each one talking at once.

"I bet we get at least a hundred responses," Rocky declared.

"A hundred?" Gwen scoffed. "I don't think there are a hundred bachelors in Deerfield."

"Of course there are," Zan replied. "Deerfield has a population of almost a hundred thousand people. Let's say that half of them, fifty thousand of them, are men."

"How do you know that?" Mary Bubnik asked.

"I read it in the paper last Sunday," Zan said. "So I figure at least ten thousand must be eligible bachelors."

"Ten thousand!" Mary Bubnik shook her head. "I don't think I can read that many letters by Saturday."

Gwen rolled her eyes. "I doubt if they'll all read our ad and respond."

"But what if they did?" Zan said dreamily. "We'd be able to pick the most truly perfect valentine ever for Annie. Wouldn't that be wonderful?"

The girls stopped in front of Hi's picture window and peered inside. Annie was still sitting on a stool at the counter, talking to Jay and Mr. Lo.

"Poor Annie," Rocky said, shaking her head. "I feel sorry for her, being forced to talk to my brother Jay."

Zan sighed. "Her life must be so lonely."

"But not for long," McGee said confidently. "When we get those letters back and pick out the perfect bachelor, Annie won't know what hit her!"

Chapter Nine

On Wednesday, Zan and Rocky went to the *Deerfield Times* to collect the responses to their personal ad. Sophie wasn't there, but she had left a note for them to go to the circulation desk. A huge canvas bag stuffed with letters was waiting for them.

"This is truly amazing!" Zan said, struggling to lift the bag off the ground.

"Maybe Mary Bubnik was right," Rocky said, as she came to Zan's aid and grabbed the other end of the sack. "Maybe there *are* ten thousand letters in here. It sure feels like it."

"The gang is going to be so excited!" The two half-carried, half-dragged the cumbersome bag down the street to the Deerfield Academy of Dance.

They paused to catch their breath, then carried their precious cargo all one hundred and two marble steps up to the entrance. By the time they reached the ballet studio offices on the third floor, both girls were huffing and puffing from their exertions.

"Are you sure no one will be in the dressing room right now?" Rocky gasped.

"I'm positive," Zan panted. "The Wednesday classes all take place between three and four. We have a whole hour to ourselves."

Rocky looked warily at the overstuffed bag of letters. "I hope that's enough time to read all these."

Zan had been right. The only person in the office was Miss Delacorte, the Russian receptionist. She greeted them with a cheery wave of her bright red scarf. "My goodness! What have you girls got in that bag, lead weights?"

"Laundry!" Rocky said, thinking fast.

"Homework!" Zan shouted at the same time.

The two girls looked at each other, and then back at a confused Miss Delacorte. "Both!"

Before Miss Delacorte could ask any more questions they scurried past her desk into the dressing room. The rest of the gang was already there, waiting. Gwen had come prepared. She'd spread out four Twinkies, several chocolate bars, a bag of M&M's, and a two-liter plastic bottle of root beer on the dressing table.

"Mail call!" Rocky announced as the two girls entered the room with their bag. She undid the draw-string and emptied the contents onto the floor in the center of the room.

"Look at all those letters!" Mary Bubnik squealed. She dropped to her knees and ran her hands through the pile. "Oh, I just *knew* Annie would be popular!"

The four other girls sat cross-legged in a circle around the mound of letters. McGee checked her watch and declared, "We have exactly forty-five min-utes until Miss Jo and Mr. Anton's classes get out. We'd better work fast."

"But not too fast," Zan cautioned. "We want to make sure we choose the absolute *perfect* valentine for Annie. We need to examine each letter carefully."

"That sounds like a line from one of your Tiffany Truenut mysteries," Gwen cracked, popping another handful of M&M's in her mouth.

"That's Tiffany True*note*," Zan corrected. "And, in a way, this is a mystery." Her eyes gleamed brightly. "Somewhere in these letters is the man of Annie's dreams. It's up to us to discover who he is."

"This is so exciting!" Mary Bubnik cooed in her soft Southern drawl. "Maybe someday I can put an ad in the paper and find my own Prince Charming."

"I already know who mine is," McGee sighed. "Zach."

"He can't be," Gwen said. "Because he's my Prince Charming."

91

"So?"

Gwen put her hands on her hips. "So bug off. I saw him first."

"It doesn't matter who saw him first," McGee said. "Zach will decide who he likes." She flipped one braid over her shoulder. "And it's *not* going to be you."

"Wanna bet?" Gwen challenged, putting her nose almost against McGee's.

"I wish you could hear how stupid you two sound," Rocky said, sticking her face between them. "Arguing over a dumb boy."

"Who are you calling stupid?" McGee made a face at Rocky.

"Come on, you guys," Mary Bubnik pleaded. "Don't fight. I just hate it when you fight."

"Besides, we really don't have the time," Zan reminded them. "We have to put on our thinking caps and figure out a system for choosing the perfect date for *Annie.*"

"Well, we can forget this one," McGee said, crumpling up the envelope she'd been holding and tossing it toward the wastebasket. As it went in, she raised both fists above her head. "Two points!"

Zan looked at her in horror. "Why did you do that?"

"He didn't send a picture," McGee explained. "So he must be ugly."

Rocky scooped up a pile of letters into her lap

and started tearing them open. "Let's start by dumping all the guys who didn't send a picture of themselves."

"Good idea." Gwen licked her fingers and scooped up an armful of envelopes. The others followed suit and within ten minutes, they had reduced the number of letters to forty. The girls stared at the pile glumly, unsure of what to do next.

"There's still so many left," Mary Bubnik fretted. "How do we find the perfect valentine?"

"Remember, he's got to be athletic," McGee reminded them.

"And intelligent," Zan added.

"He should like hot fudge sundaes," Gwen said, reaching for a Twinkie. "A guy can't be all bad if he likes ice cream."

"I think he should know how to defend himself," Rocky advised, giving the air a karate chop. "Just in case they meet some thugs on one of their dates, and he has to protect her."

"Well, I just think he should be nice," Mary Bubnik said, folding her arms across her chest. "How hard is that to find?"

"There's got to be at least one guy in this pile who's all of those things," Rocky said confidently.

"Now all we have to do is find him," McGee sighed.

Zan leaned forward and sorted the letters into five equal stacks. "Why don't we each take a pile, read the letters, then switch stacks until each of us has looked at them all? Then we'll each pick our favorite and vote."

"Good thinking." McGee anxiously checked her watch. "We have exactly thirty minutes left before this room is filled with a bunch of twinkle-toes, so let's work fast."

Each girl grabbed a pile and found a special spot in the room to set to work. Gwen sat behind the freestanding mirror, where she usually changed into her ballet clothes. Mary Bubnik plopped down in the chair next to the row of lockers. Rocky and McGee sat on the floor using a bench as a table. Zan sat at the dressing table and leaned each picture up against the mirror as she read the letters.

For the next fifteen minutes, the only sound that could be heard was soft piano music coming from the dance studios, the shuffle of papers, and occasionally the crumpling of Gwen's M&M bag. This was serious business.

"OK, time's up!" McGee called. As the other girls clustered around her, she held her selection up in one hand. "Everyone got their perfect guy?"

"You bet!" Rocky gave a thumbs-up sign. The rest nodded enthusiastically.

"OK, I'll go first." McGee held up her picture. "Meet Robert. He loves skiing, sledding, *and*" — she wiggled her eyebrows — "hockey! I think he's the perfect choice." She sat down on the floor, confident that the others would agree with her.

"I don't think he's half as perfect as Stan," Rocky said, flipping her photo into the air. "He has a third-degree black belt in Tae Kwon Do." She moved around the circle, shoving his picture in everyone's face. "Face it, you can't get much cooler than ol' Stan."

Zan stood up. "We can't forget that intelligence is terribly important. Matthew Peabody is a history professor at Deerfield College. I'm sure Annie would find him truly fascinating and —"

"You'd have to be fascinating to have a name like François," Gwen interrupted. "Look here, Frank is a *cordon bleu* chef at the Deerfield Hilton." She held up his picture. There was a large smear of chocolate over the corner. "Oops, I did that." Gwen giggled and wiped the picture clean on her parka. "Annie would never be hungry if she married François."

"Annie's a dancer," McGee protested. "She doesn't need to get fat with your chef."

"Well, she doesn't need to break her leg skiing with Robert, either," Gwen retorted.

"Please!" Zan said, stepping between them. "We only have a few minutes left to work on Operation Annie. Don't start fighting now."

"What do y'all think of Ryan?" Mary Bubnik asked, waving her photo in the middle of them. "Isn't he perfect?"

"What does Ryan do?" Gwen demanded, putting her hands on her hips.

Mary Bubnik shrugged. "I don't know. I didn't read any of those silly letters."

"Then how do you know he's perfect?" McGee wondered.

"Because of his face." She held the picture under her chin. "Doesn't he have a nice smile? And look at those puppy dog eyes!"

"Let me see the letter." Gwen snatched the envelope out of Mary Bubnik's other hand and quickly scanned the letter. "He's got puppy dog eyes because he's a *dogcatcher*."

"Oh, no!" Mary dropped his picture like it was poison. "I can't believe it."

"Not only does he catch poor helpless dogs, but he also likes to hunt." Gwen folded the letter back up and added, "And he says, in extra big letters, that he's sorry but he can't dance."

"This is terrible!" Mary Bubnik slumped to the floor in despair. "And he had such a nice face, too." She searched through her pile and held up another picture. "I guess I'll have to go with my second choice then." She quickly checked the letter that accompanied the picture and said, "Ethan is a computer programmer."

The girls stared at Ethan's picture and then back at their own.

"I don't know about you guys," Zan said, scooping

96

the other letters back into the canvas bag, "but I think we are going to need some outside help."

"We could ask Miss Delacorte," Gwen suggested. "She knows Annie really well."

"Or some of the other dancers from the *corps de ballet*," McGee added.

Rocky shook her head. "We want Annie to be surprised. They might tell her."

Zan put one finger to her lips. "We need someone who is truly wise and totally trustworthy."

"Well, there's only one person I know who fits that description," Mary Bubnik said.

"Who?" the others asked together.

Mary's face burst into a big grin. "Why, Hi, of course."

"Of course!" Rocky pulled Mary to her feet and gave her a bear hug.

"Come on, let's go," McGee urged.

Gwen had already put on her coat. "Maybe we can get Hi to fix one of his specials. I'm starved."

McGee checked her watch. "Hey, we'd better get out of here fast, before we're invaded."

The girls scrambled out of the dressing room and down the steps of the Academy just minutes before the classes let out. All four of them carried the canvas bag between them. They made a funny sight as they crossed the street to Hi Lo's.

Gwen, who was in front, pushed open the glass door with her foot and the tinkling bell announced their arrival. "Hi, Hi!" she shouted as they stumbled into the tiny restaurant.

"Greetings and salutations!" Mr. Lo called from behind the counter. He spotted the bag they were carrying and said, "If that's laundry you're carrying, you've come to the wrong place. My family quit that business years ago."

Mary Bubnik giggled. "These are letters. We want you to look at them."

Gwen nodded. "We really need your help, Hi."

"We're truly desperate," Zan added.

"But you have to be sworn to secrecy," Rocky said.

Hi bowed stiffly from the waist. "You have my word of honor, as a *samurai* warrior."

McGee's green eyes widened. "You're a *samurai?*"

"No," Hi admitted with a grin, "but it sounds better than giving you my word as a Boy Scout." His smile spread dozens of tiny wrinkles across his face.

Each girl carefully set her photograph and letter in front of him on the counter.

"One of these guys is going to be the date for someone we all know," McGee explained. "We just can't decide which one."

"We want you to choose," Zan said.

"I see." He adjusted the wire-rimmed glasses perched on the tip of his nose and peered down at

98

the photos. After a moment, he shook his head. "This kind of decision requires a good deal of careful thought and —" He slapped his palm on the counter. "One of my Valentine's Day Specials!"

"All right!" Gwen shouted jubilantly, hopping onto one of the red leather stools. "I hope it's pink and got something to do with ice cream."

"We shall see." Hi disappeared into the kitchen, and they could hear the sound of the refrigerator opening and the whirring of a blender.

"It's a good thing you suggested we come here," Gwen said to Mary. "Otherwise we might have missed out on a Hi Holiday Special."

"I wonder if this one will have a secret ingredient," Mary mused. "Like peanut butter."

McGee groaned. "I hope not!"

The girls never knew what to expect with one of Hi's "specials." Sometimes they were an incredibly delicious surprise and other times they were just plain weird. They'd learned to eat first, and ask questions later.

Moments later the elderly man emerged from his kitchen carrying a large round tray laden with tall glasses filled to the brim with a creamy pink substance.

"In honor of Valentine's Day," he announced proudly, "I present to you my 'Roses are Red' strawberry milkshakes."

There were soft cries of delight as Hi placed a frosty glass in front of each girl. "Now you enjoy these while I peruse the pictures."

Rocky was the first to dip her long-handled spoon into the frothy concoction. "Outstanding!"

"Heavenly!" Gwen cooed.

"Truly wonderful," Zan murmured, wiping a little milk moustache off of her lip with her paper napkin.

Mary Bubnik and McGee were too busy slurping theirs down to comment.

Meanwhile, Hi carefully examined each photograph. He read the letters one by one, then placed them back in their envelopes. Then he stared at the pictures again, thoughtfully rubbing his chin with his fingers.

"Well? What do you think?" McGee asked as soon as she'd finished her shake.

"Yeah," Gwen said, with a loud slurp. "The suspense is killing me."

Hi looked at the girls, then back at the pictures. "It is most definitely a difficult decision."

Rocky set her glass down. "You're telling me."

"But, you know," Hi said softly, "I think that, if I were going on a date, I'd rather choose the person myself."

The phone rang from inside the kitchen and Hi said, "Excuse me one moment, please."

"You know, Hi's got a good point," Rocky said as soon as the little man left the room.

"But how can we have Annie choose?" Gwen asked. "I mean, we can't exactly show her the pictures and tell her to pick one. She'd probably say no to the whole idea."

McGee slid off her stool and paced back and forth. "What if we sent her the pictures and letters, saying that they were secret admirers that wanted to meet her?"

"That would sound too fishy to me," Gwen said. "She'd know something was up right away."

"Well, we can't stop now," Mary Bubnik moaned. "Annie's got to have a valentine!"

Suddenly Zan's brown eyes lit up. "I've got it. What if we have them all meet Annie face-to-face?"

"But she'd never agree to that," Gwen objected.

"She wouldn't have to agree," McGee said with a sly smile. "We'd just need some excuse to introduce the guys to her, then we could tell by her reaction which guy was Mr. Right."

"But where should they meet?" Mary Bubnik asked.

"Good question," McGee admitted. "We sure struck out at the doctor's office."

"Why not here?" Gwen suggested. "She comes in all the time for noodles and vegetables."

Rocky shook her head. "Too chancy. We could never be sure of the exact time she'd walk in."

Mary Bubnik took one last sip of her shake. "Well, I don't see why we can't just invite the guys to our

Valentine's Day party at the studio. Annie has to be there, and there'll be lots of other guests, too."

Each girl slowly turned to face Mary in amazement.

"Of course," Zan whispered. "It's practically perfect."

"Practically? It *is* perfect," Rocky said in amazement. "Mary Bubnik, you're a genius!"

"Aw, shucks, you guys!" Mary said shyly.

"Here's the plan," McGee said. "Now, each of us will call up our choice during the week and set a rendezvous for Saturday during the party."

"We'll have them come at different times," Rocky added.

"And then we can introduce them to Annie as a relative," Gwen finished.

Zan pulled out her lavender pad and started writing furiously. "We'll give each bachelor fifteen minutes."

"That should be more than enough time," Mary Bubnik reasoned. "After all, love at first sight only takes a second."

"Now, one last thing." Zan put down her pen and folded her hands. "What should we wear for the Valentine's Day party?"

"Wear?" Rocky repeated. "Our leotards and tights, of course. What are you planning to do?"

Zan flushed and looked down at her lap. "Well, I thought, since it was Valentine's Day —"

McGee nodded. "And a party, and all—"

"And since we're giving out cards," Mary Bubnik added.

"And eating fancy food," Gwen said, taking another slurp of her soda.

Rocky folded her arms across her chest and said sarcastically, "And since *Zachary-Thackary* is going to be there, you're all planning to make fools of yourselves by dressing up."

"Who, us?" the four girls cried indignantly. "Never!"

Chapter Ten

Rocky rode the bus from the air base into downtown Deerfield on Valentine's Day. She sat in the back row, carefully cradling a pale pink envelope in her arms. Rocky had spent her entire allowance on that one valentine. It had been so expensive that she'd had no money left over to buy cards for her friends.

"MacArthur Street," the bus driver sang out. Rocky pulled the cord, and the big city bus rolled to a stop. The doors opened with a swoosh, and she was suddenly standing in front of the Academy.

Rocky checked her watch. She was twenty minutes early and the marble steps leading up to the Academy entrance were completely deserted.

She had planned to tell her friends about the valentine, her secret crush, her tears — everything. But as the minutes ticked by she lost her nerve. How can I tell them? she thought. They'll never understand. They'll probably make fun of me!

Rocky tucked the pale pink envelope inside her jacket and hurried up the steps to the Deerfield Academy of Dance. "It'll have to stay my secret."

"Where is everybody?" Gwen asked after McGee's mother had dropped them off in front of Hillberry Hall. She squinted down the street. Gwen had taken her glasses off and carefully applied mascara to her pale lashes. It made her eyes stand out, but she couldn't see three feet in front of her. "Is that them?"

McGee followed the direction that Gwen was pointing and burst out laughing. "Boy, you must be blind. That's two old ladies standing by a No Parking sign."

"Well, they're both short, and from this angle, that sign looks a whole lot like Zan in her lavender beret."

"I think you should put your glasses back on," McGee said. "You could get hurt."

Gwen's eyes widened. "I can't. What if we run into Zach? I don't want him to think I'm a four-eyes."

"He saw you last week and the week before with your glasses on. What difference does it make?"

"Maybe he forgot." Gwen put her hands on her hips. "Besides, he saw you with braids and now you look like you stuck your finger in a socket."

"I do?" McGee's hands flew to her hair. She and her older sister had spent two hours putting her long chestnut hair in curlers. That morning her mother had helped her comb it out and put a lot of gooey styling gel and hair spray on it. "Sara said this mousse stuff is what everyone is wearing."

"That may be true, but don't let Zach near it." Gwen reached up and tapped McGee's hair with her fingers. "He could break his hand. It's like cement."

"Geez Louise, Gwen!" McGee pushed Gwen's hand away. "Zach's going to look at it, not punch it!"

"When the others arrive, let's not mention our getting made up for Zach. They'll make fun of us," Gwen said.

McGee nodded. "Especially Rocky. But it's kind of hard to miss. I mean, no one has ever seen you with your glasses off and wearing makeup."

"That's true, and you've never curled your hair before."

McGee bit her lip in thought. "We could tell them our mothers are taking us out to dinner after the class party."

"Good idea." Gwen and McGee's mothers were best friends and for several years had forced their daughters to get dressed up and attend teas or fashion shows with them. It was always pure agony for the girls. "I'm sure they'll believe that."

"Actually," McGee said, her voice suddenly sounding strange, "I don't think we have to worry about telling them anything."

"What do you mean?"

McGee pointed over Gwen's shoulder. "Look."

"You know I can't see a thing," Gwen hissed.

"Put your glasses on," McGee whispered. "This is worth looking at." When Gwen hesitated, McGee added, "Zach's nowhere to be seen."

Gwen dug into the coat pocket of her parka and slipped her wire-rim glasses on her nose. She spun to look where McGee had pointed and nearly choked.

Mary Bubnik was teetering down the sidewalk on high heels. Zan slouched beside her, trying to keep her knees bent as she walked. Each time Mary Bubnik stumbled, Zan would catch Mary by the arm and lift her up.

"Look at Mary's face," McGee giggled.

Mary Bubnik had used a dark brown pencil to color in her eyebrows and then painstakingly drawn dozens of little eyelashes all around her eyes. She had big red circles of blush on her cheeks and the same color smeared across her lips.

"She looks like Raggedy Ann," Gwen quipped.

"No kidding," McGee agreed. "But look at Zan. She looks so old."

Zan had swept her black hair to one side in a

107

sparkly clip. Matching earrings dangled from her ears and her makeup was perfectly done. She looked like a model from a fashion magazine.

"I wonder why she's walking hunched over like that," Gwen mused.

"I think she wants to impress Zach, but she's afraid she might be too tall for him."

"Happy Valentine's Day, y'all!" Mary Bubnik called when she spotted them. "Boy, do you two look nice."

Gwen swallowed the urge to tell Mary the truth — that she looked ridiculous. Instead she forced herself to say, "So do you."

"Where's Rocky?" Mary Bubnik asked, tripping over her heels and falling against McGee.

"Hey, watch it, Mary," McGee said, helping her regain her balance. "You could hurt yourself."

"It's these high heels," Mary Bubnik whispered. "I've never worn them before. Can you tell?"

McGee and Gwen exchanged quick looks, then answered exaggeratedly, "Nooooo!"

Zan looked around cautiously, then straightened her knees. "Someone tell me if you see Zach. I can't hold this for long, it's too painful."

"Wait till Rocky sees us," Gwen said, shaking her head. "She'll never let us live this down."

"I think we look nice," Mary Bubnik said, patting her hair. "Besides, Rocky probably won't even notice."

"Where is Rocky?" McGee wondered. "You don't think she'd skip class today, do you?"

"And miss the party?" Mary Bubnik gasped. "Oh, that'd be awful!"

"Besides, she knows how important this day is," Zan said. "After all, today is the day Annie will choose the man of her dreams."

"Maybe she got tied up in traffic," Gwen suggested. "I never realized how far she had to come until we went to her house on the air base."

"That's true," Zan said softly. "Should we wait for her here, or go on inside?"

"I thought we were going to exchange our valentines before the party," Mary said.

"Let's do ours," McGee suggested, "and maybe by that time, Rocky will have gotten here."

"OK." Gwen reached into her blue dance bag and pulled out four cards. She put one of them back, then held up the rest. "Here's mine."

The other three quickly got theirs, and the girls exchanged cards.

Each girl had chosen cards that reflected her personality. Mary Bubnik's cards were of stuffed animals with little pockets where a tiny paper heart could be slipped in and out. McGee's had circus acrobats on them, doing cartwheels through heart-shaped rings. Zan's were of a mime gazing romantically at the crescent moon. Gwen's cards each had a slender piece of chocolate, cut in a heart shape, taped to the inside.

They oohed and aahed over each one. Finally the only envelopes left were for Rocky. McGee glanced at her watch and grimaced. "Gee, guys, maybe she really isn't coming. If we don't get upstairs, we're going to be late for dance class."

"Dance class!" the others all shouted at once. Immediately Zan bent her knees. Gwen removed her glasses, and Mary hurriedly pinned a bow in her hair — crooked.

"I wonder if Zach will be there today," Mary giggled as they hurried up to the second floor of the building, where the studios were.

"He'd better be," McGee said, patting her stiff hair. "I don't want to have gone to all this trouble for nothing."

The girls stepped into the lobby of the academy and waved to Miss Delacorte at the reception desk.

"Happy Valentine's Day!" they chorused.

"These are from us," Mary announced, dropping four envelopes onto the elderly lady's desk.

"Oh, how lovely!" The elderly lady was wearing a bright red bow around her gray hair, with little candy hearts dangling from it.. "Thank you, girls, so much." Miss Delacorte pointed at the studio and added, "You'd better hurry, or you'll be late."

"See you at the party!" Mary Bubnik called back. As they passed Studio B, McGee grabbed Zan by

110

the arm and whispered, "Look! There's Zach. He's warming up at the *barre.*"

"Let me see." Mary Bubnik struggled to peek over Gwen's shoulder. "He's even cuter this week than he was last week."

"Look at the Bunheads," Zan said under her breath. "They've truly outdone themselves this time."

Reflected in the mirror were Courtney and Page, standing at opposite ends of the room, kicking furiously into the air. They were obviously still ignoring each other. Courtney wore a shiny black leotard that was cut high up on the legs, with long sleeves that tapered to points at her wrists. Page's leotard was sleeveless and had a tiny skirt. It sparkled every time she moved.

"They look fantastic," Mary Bubnik whispered.

"Yeah," Gwen muttered. "But if they're not careful, they're going to pull something."

"Look at how high Page is doing her *grand battements,*" McGee said. "She could break her nose."

"They're really trying to show off for Zach," Mary Bubnik said. "And he doesn't even seem to notice them."

Zach was methodically working through his *pliés* and *relevés.* As they watched, he rested his leg upon the *barre* and bent forward, touching his head to his knee.

"Ouch! That has got to hurt," Gwen said with a grimace.

111

"You know, that new girl is pretty good," McGee murmured. "Look at her over in the corner."

Trisha Miller was doing the same exercises as Zach and each of her movements was soft and graceful. She raised up on half-point, released her hold on the *barre,* and balanced for a very long time.

"That's perfectly beautiful," Zan sighed. "I wish I could do that."

"We can," Gwen said defensively. "We just need a little more practice."

"We'd better change," McGee warned, "or we'll miss the class and the party."

"I need to sort through the rest of my valentines," Mary Bubnik said.

The girls scurried toward the dressing room. McGee threw back the long black curtain, and all four girls froze in their tracks.

Standing in front of them was the most shocking sight they'd ever seen. Rocky was in the corner, doing her warm-ups. She hadn't heard them come in.

"Where's her red jacket?" Gwen hissed.

"And high-top tennis shoes?" McGee added.

"And what happened to her wonderfully wild hair?" Zan cried.

Rocky heard their voices and turned to look at them. Her dark, curly hair was pulled tightly into a bun at the top of her head. Not a hair was out of place. She was dressed in a brand-new black leotard with long sleeves and vee neck. Without a word, she grabbed her jacket and raced past them out of the room.

"Oh, no!" Mary Bubnik's hands flew to her face in horror. "Rocky's become a Bunhead!"

Chapter Eleven

When the gang entered the ballet studio, Rocky had already taken a place at the *barre* between Courtney Clay and Trisha Miller. Before the girls could say anything to her, the studio door opened and Annie Springer came into the room.

"Happy Valentine's Day!" their teacher greeted them. She'd gotten into the spirit of the holiday and braided a bright red ribbon into her hair The color added a bright accent to her usual uniform of black leotard and dance skirt. "This is going to be a fun class."

"Fun?" Gwen gasped. "Right now it feels like pure agony."

"Maybe if you took off your grandmother's girdle, you'd feel better," McGee whispered.

Gwen shot her a warning look. "Shhh! Zach might hear you."

"All he has to do is look at you to know."

Gwen looked at her reflection in the mirror and nearly fainted. She'd crammed her body into the full-length girdle moments ago, in an attempt to look her absolute best for Zach. Her waist did look tiny but the tight girdle made her hips bulge out at the edges. The metal stays dug into her armpits so she had to hold her arms out to the side. The pain she felt showed clearly on her face.

"We'll start with a few *pliés*, just to warm up," Annie instructed. "Then we'll pass out our valentines."

Giggles went around the room as every girl glanced shyly at Zach. He was busy pulling up his socks and didn't seem to notice the attention he was attracting.

Mrs. Bruce hit a chord on the piano, and the class began their exercises. Annie walked around the room, smiling and nodding at her students. When her back was turned, McGee hissed, "Look at Rocky over there with the Bunheads. What's she trying to prove, anyway?"

Gwen didn't answer. She was in too much pain. The girdle had begun to cut off her circulation and little spots danced in front of her eyes.

"Well, if you ask me," Zan whispered, "I think she's trying to impress Zach."

"*Impress* him?" McGee repeated. "But she's the one who's called him names."

"And laughed at him," Gwen added.

"And tripped him," Mary Bubnik said.

"My point exactly," Zan smiled. "Rocky's in love."

"Love!" The girls looked at Rocky a little differently this time. Rocky was concentrating as hard as she could on doing the warm-ups correctly. Every now and then she would sneak a glance at Zach's direction, to see if he noticed her.

"I don't believe it," McGee declared, shaking her head.

"Who would have ever thought it?" Mary Bubnik murmured.

"I think I'm going to be sick," Gwen wheezed. "Rocky's become a Bunhead, and I've become a tubesteak in tights."

Annie clapped her hands to signal the end of the warm-ups. "Attention, everyone. Mrs. Bruce will play some music, and I want you to move in time with it. When it's fast — *allegro* — I want you to scurry along the floor. When it's slow — *adagio* — I want to see long, graceful movements." She smiled and added, "Now here's the fun part. Those of you who brought valentines can use this music to deliver your cards to each other."

Rocky skipped to the corner where she had set

116

her red satin jacket on the floor. She checked the inside pocket to make sure the precious card was still there. It was, and her heart beat faster just thinking about giving it to Zach.

Mrs. Bruce began to play and the room swirled with activity. Courtney led the dancing as she delivered little gold boxes of Godiva chocolates to her special friends. Of course, she ignored the gang, dancing right past them with a smug smile on her face. The smile disappeared when she snubbed Page Tuttle and pointedly handed a large box to Trisha Miller.

"Look, Courtney gave that new girl a box of chocolates," Gwen whispered enviously.

"That's because Trisha took ballet in New York," Zan explained.

"And because she's awfully nice," Mary Bubnik added.

Then Courtney picked up the largest box of all and, with a deep, low curtsy, placed it in Zach's hands. He seemed shocked by the extravagance of the gift, but nothing prepared him for what came next. One by one, each girl in the class danced up to him and handed him a valentine.

"Come on, guys," McGee said, "it's either now, or never." She led Gwen, Zan, and Mary Bubnik in an impromptu snake dance around the floor. Each gave an envelope to every member of their class, including the Bunheads. Courtney looked shocked, but said nothing when she received hers. Page Tuttle forced a tight smile. Alice Westcott just looked confused.

Then McGee danced them over to Zach, who hadn't moved a muscle. The gang threw themselves into their presentation, but nothing worked out right. Attempting to do a deep curtsy, Mary Bubnik wobbled and fell backwards onto her bottom. McGee promptly tripped over Mary's outstretched legs. Gwen could only manage a stiff bow from the waist. Even then the girdle dug deeply into her stomach. As she handed Zach his valentine, she croaked, "Here . . . *ouch!*"

Zan was so busy trying to look shorter than the others that, when she did finally straighten out her legs, her joints made a loud popping sound. There were audible hoots of laughter from Alice and Courtney.

Meanwhile, Zach simply stared at the floor. He was so embarrassed by all the attention that the tips of his ears turned bright red.

Mrs. Bruce sped up the music, and McGee hissed to the others, "Let's get out of here."

With a sinking feeling, Rocky watched her friends skip toward her. They'd just made complete fools of themselves in front of Zach and now they were going to embarrass her, too.

"Happy Valentine's Day, Rocky," Mary Bubnik

said. "Even though you've become a Bunhead, I still like you."

"We know why you did it," McGee added with a wink, "and it's OK."

Rocky didn't know what to say. Suddenly the music changed to a slow, beautiful melody, and Zach stepped away from the *barre*. He danced slowly across the room.

"He's coming this way," Mary Bubnik whispered.

Rocky's heart started pounding. She couldn't take her eyes off him. Zach seemed to be heading straight for her. She bent down and, removing the pink envelope from beneath her jacket, stepped away from the *barre*. Taking a slow, long step, Rocky danced out to meet him.

She decided to present his valentine to him in an *arabesque*. Now he was only a step away from her. Rocky ducked her head down, glanced at her valentine, then stretched her arms forward, with her leg extended high behind her.

But Zach was gone! He'd danced right past her.

A gasp from the group made Rocky spin around. She watched in horror as Zach pulled out a tiny white envelope from his belt and handed it to Trisha Miller. She took it and, with a dazzling smile, curtsied beautifully to thank him.

Rocky wanted to sink into the floor, but she forced herself to stay cool. The music was still playing and, keeping her chin up, she danced toward the door of the studio. Rocky felt that, if she could just get through that door, she'd never come back again.

Most of the class was in a state of shock. Courtney and Page looked flabbergasted. Nobody had dreamed Zach might have a crush on the new girl. Looks of disappointment were everywhere. But the gang could only think of Rocky.

"Look at her face," Zan said. "I think she's going to cry."

"How humiliating!" Gwen said as they watched Rocky move stiffly toward the door.

"I'd want to die," McGee said sympathetically.

Just before Rocky reached the door, her chin began to quiver. She dropped her pose and ran headlong out of the room.

"Come on," Gwen said. "We've got to help her!"

When they ran into the dressing room, Rocky was throwing her shoes at her reflection in the mirror. The beautiful pink valentine lay discarded on the floor. She tugged the rubber band out of her hair and her wild, black curls exploded into their normal disarray.

"Hey, Rocky," McGee said, "chill out."

Rocky spun around angrily. "Leave me alone!"

McGee folded her arms across her chest. "I can't believe you'd fall for a boy. I thought you said boys are a pain."

"They are," Rocky said, wiping her eyes with the back of her hand. "Most of the time."

"I had no idea you liked Zach," Mary Bubnik said.

"Yeah, you sure didn't act like it," Gwen added.

"Well, what did you want me to do?" Rocky retorted. "Dress up like you guys, and make a fool of myself?"

"Well, tripping a guy and laughing at him whenever he performs isn't exactly the way to his heart," Gwen said.

"I'm surprised he didn't deck you," McGee chuckled.

"Well, if you're so smart, you can have him. I'm getting out of this dump. I'm going to get my jacket, and you'll never have to look at me again."

With that, she stomped out of the dressing room and back into the studio. Luckily, punch and cookies had been served and most of the class were gathered around the refreshment table. The dancers from the other class had joined the party and now the room was quite crowded.

Keeping her eyes dead ahead, Rocky went straight for her jacket. She scooped it up and turned to leave, only to find McGee and the gang.

"Aw, come on, Rocky," McGee pleaded, "you can't let a boy break up our friendship."

"Yeah," Mary Bubnik said, her big blue eyes watering dangerously. "That would just be awful."

"I mean, look at it this way," Gwen pointed out logically. "All of us liked Zach, and none of us got him."

"Right," McGee added. "Not even the Bunheads."

Rocky looked over at Courtney and Page. They were sulking in the corner, not talking to anyone or each other.

McGee handed her four envelopes and grinned. "Besides, you wouldn't want us to waste these valentines we got for you, would you?"

Rocky looked at the envelopes in her hand and swallowed hard. "You guys, I — I have a confession to make."

"What?" Zan asked.

"I spent all of my money on that valentine for Zach, and I didn't get you a thing."

No one said anything for a moment. Then Zan reached out and touched Rocky on the shoulder. "Friends don't need to give each other presents," Zan said softly. "It's just being friends that matters the most."

Mary Bubnik nodded. "Being a friend means sharing and doing things together like" — she paused and crossed her hands over her heart — "Operation Annie."

The others automatically crossed their hands over their hearts. Then their eyes popped open wide and they screeched as one, "Operation Annie! What time is it?"

Just then Miss Delacorte appeared at the studio door. Five strange gentlemen stood behind her.

"Excuse me, please," she announced to the room. "But these men are look-ink for a beautiful dancer, who wants excitement, adventure, and free dinners."

"Oh, no!"

"I think I'm going to faint." Gwen threw herself on the floor, hoping against hope that she would pass out. The others wished they could do the same.

Chapter Twelve

Gwen opened her eyes very slowly. All she could see were concerned faces staring down at her. It worked! she thought to herself. They think I actually fainted. Now maybe they'll forget about the bachelors all showing up at once, and we can get out of here.

Off to one side she could hear Mary Bubnik saying, "You see, Annie, our plan was to have you meet them today and fall madly in love."

Gwen groaned and squeezed her eyes shut again. Rocky saw the movement, grabbed a glass of punch and splashed it in Gwen's face.

"Oh, yuck!" Gwen squealed, sitting straight up. "Why'd you have to do that?"

"Because you're in this, too," Rocky muttered between clenched teeth. "No fair faking a faint to get out of it."

When the crowd saw that Gwen was all right, they went back to chatting and eating. Everyone except Annie Springer. She stood in front of the girls and shook her head in dismay. "You know you girls should never have done what you did."

"We know," Zan said ruefully. "And we're truly sorry."

"What do you think your parents would do if they heard about this?"

"Probably ground us for a week," McGee mumbled.

Rocky gulped. She knew that if her father found out, he would probably ground her for the rest of sixth grade. Maybe for all of junior high school.

Annie smiled. "Well I'm not going to tell your parents, but I hope you understand that what you did was wrong."

"But we were only looking out for you," Mary Bubnik protested feebly. "We didn't want you to be a lonely old maid."

"Mary, I'm not an old maid!" Annie exclaimed with a laugh. "I am nineteen years old and perfectly capable of finding my own boyfriend." A smile crept across her face. "Which I have done. . . ."

"You have?" they all asked. "Who?"

Annie gestured toward the studio door. There, leaning against the doorjam with an amused twinkle in his eye, stood Jay Garcia.

"My brother?" Rocky cried. "Oh, gross!"

Jay sauntered over and playfully ruffled Rocky's hair. "Hi, squirt! Surprised?"

"I'm in shock," Rocky said. "How could this happen?"

"Remember that day you fainted?"

Rocky nodded. That was the day Plan Two had failed because Jay had interfered. How could she forget?

"Well, Annie and I just seemed to hit it off instantly." He looked at Gwen and scratched his head. "By the way, you guys sure do a lot of fainting. I think you should really cut out that dieting stuff."

Gwen, who was still sitting on the floor, moaned, "It's not the dieting, it's this, this thing I have on! Someone get me out of it!"

"Zan, would you help me with her?" McGee asked. "I hope somebody brought a can opener."

"Very funny," Gwen retorted. "Remind me to put glue in your ice skates sometime."

They pulled Gwen to her feet and helped her walk to the dressing room. Mary Bubnik looked up at Annie and asked timidly, "Does this mean you don't like us anymore, Annie?"

Annie looked down at her and smiled. "Of course

not. I'd just appreciate it if you'd leave me out of any dating schemes in the future, OK?"

"It's a deal!"

"Come on," Annie said, taking Mary by the arm. "Let's get some more punch and cookies."

That left Rocky standing alone with her brother. She didn't know what to say, so she stuck out her hand and murmured, "Congratulations."

Jay shook it. "Thanks."

"You wouldn't have been my first choice to be Annie's valentine," Rocky continued, "but that's only because you're my brother."

Jay looked confused. "Valentine? Is that what day this is?"

"Well, of course," Rocky replied. "Why do you think we're having this dumb party, and drinking pink punch?"

Jay slapped his hand against his forehead. "I forgot all about it. Annie just said there was going to be a little get-together today. She didn't mention Valentine's Day at all."

"She probably didn't want you to think she was hinting around."

Jay slumped against the wall. "Boy, do I feel like a jerk!"

Rocky folded her arms across her chest indignantly. "You should!"

"Maybe if I hurry, I can find a flower shop, or

something," Jay mumbled, starting to move toward the door.

"Wait a minute." Rocky grabbed his sleeve. "You can't leave the party. That wouldn't be nice."

"I know," he replied, "but what else can I do? I've got to give her something."

"I've got an idea," Rocky said suddenly. "Come with me."

Taking him by the hand, she led Jay through the crowd and out of the studio into the lobby. At the door to the girl's dressing room, she stopped and said, "Wait here." Then she pulled back the curtain and stepped inside.

At the far side of the room, Gwen was holding onto the sides of the dressing table while Zan and McGee struggled to yank the girdle off her.

"Pull!" McGee ordered.

"You're strangling me!" Gwen screamed.

"Let me help," Rocky said, running over to join them. She grabbed a hold of the girdle and then nodded to McGee. "Pull!"

After two mighty heaves they managed to get it past her shoulders and around her neck. Finally Gwen tugged it over her head and fell against the dressing table, gasping, "Free at last!"

"What should we do with this?" McGee pointed to the elastic girdle laying on the floor.

"Burn it!" Gwen shrieked. "I never want to see that instrument of torture again."

The curtain burst open and an excited Mary Bubnik dashed into the room. "You guys would not *believe* what is happening out there," she gushed.

"Not another disaster!" Zan moaned.

"What'd we do this time?" McGee asked.

"No, no, this is great!" Mary Bubnik sat down on
the bench and said, "Remember our bachelors?"

"How could we forget?" Rocky muttered.

"They all decided to stay, and they're having a
great time." She wiggled her eyebrows mysteriously.
"I think they're even meeting some bachelorettes."

"This I gotta see!" McGee led Gwen and Zan out
of the room, with Mary Bubnik giggling after them.

As soon as they were gone, Rocky got down
on her hands and knees and searched for the pale
pink envelope. After a few minutes, she found it
underneath the dressing table, unharmed. She
was glad she hadn't written Zach's name on the
outside.

She hugged it to herself for a long moment. Then
Rocky hurried back to her brother, who was waiting
impatiently outside the curtained dressing room.

"What's this?" he asked as she placed the envelope in his hands.

"A valentine for Annie," Rocky said. She kicked
at the floor with the toe of her shoe, and added, "I
got it for someone else, but that didn't work out."

Jay removed the card from the envelope and held
it up in the light. When he opened it, the inside

129

expanded into a delicate fold-out of a beautiful ballerina leaping over the moon. She held a star in her
hand, and her lacy white dress streamed behind her
like the tail of a comet.

"With you — anything is possible," Jay read softly.
He looked down at Rocky and said, "It's signed, 'Your
secret admirer.' "

"So write your name under that," Rocky said
gruffly. "She'll never know."

Jay slowly put the card back in the envelope, then
held it out to her. "I can't take this."

"Don't be a jerk," Rocky said. "Go on, give it to
her. I'm not going to need it, ever!"

Jay cupped her chin in his hand and lifted her
face to look at him. "You may not need it now," he
said softly, "but when you get a little older, the guys
better watch out, because you're going to be a heart-
breaker."

Rocky was so touched by his words that she
punched him on the shoulder. "Aw, get out of here."

Jay grinned at her, then turned and went back
into the studio. Rocky watched him go, trying to
master the jumble of feelings she had inside of her.
Finally she went to look for her pals.

They were clustered by the door, whispering ex-
citedly.

"I think it's a fantastic idea," Mary Bubnik was
saying.

"What are you guys jabbering about?" Rocky asked gruffly.

"Our new dating service," Gwen replied. "We'll call it Cupids-On-Call."

"Dating service? Are you out of your mind?" Rocky exclaimed. "After the disaster that happened today, how can you even think that?"

"But that's the point, Rocky," Zan said. "It's not a disaster. Every one of our eligible bachelors has found a valentine. Matthew Peabody turned out to be ages older than the photo he sent, but he's just the right age for Miss Delacorte. And his specialty is *Russian* history."

"And Robert, Jason, and Ethan are all flirting with dancers from the company." Gwen pointed to the bachelors, each one clutching a glass of punch and laughing merrily with one of the ballerinas.

"François is the only one who really didn't find anyone," McGee confessed.

"Are you kidding?" Gwen said. "He found the food table, and it looks like it suits him just fine." They all watched as François, the gourmet, made his way down the line of treats, piling cookies onto a paper plate.

Rocky shook her head. "But I don't see how you could run a dating service. None of these meetings were planned."

"What about Jay and Annie?" Zan said. "We arranged that match."

"That's right," McGee said. "If you hadn't pretended to faint, they probably never would have met."

"Now, don't blame it all on me," Rocky protested.

"Who's blaming you?" Gwen said. "I think they're perfect for each other."

As they watched, Jay led Annie by the hand over to the grand piano by the window. The golden afternoon light made Annie's eyes sparkle with a special brilliance. She opened the pink envelope and gasped with joy. Annie wrapped her arms around Jay's neck and hugged him. With a laugh, he lifted her up off her feet and spun her in a circle, pausing long enough to wink in Rocky's direction.

A wonderful warm feeling flowed through Rocky's entire body as she returned his smile. "You know? I think you're right. They *are* perfect for each other."

"So what about Cupids-On-Call?" Mary Bubnik asked, returning to the subject at hand.

"I still think it's a bad idea," Rocky declared. "I mean, boys mean nothing but trouble. Look at what happened to me. I almost let one break up our friendship."

There was a moment of silence as the five friends pondered that awful thought. Finally Zan said, "I think we should make a solemn vow right now, never to let a boy come between us."

She held out her hand and Gwen rested hers upon it. "No matter how cute," Gwen said.

"Or nice," Mary Bubnik said.

"Or athletic," McGee added.

"Our friendship will always come first." Rocky gripped the others' hands, and the five friends smiled at each other.

"Excuse me?" a voice interrupted from behind them. Standing in the doorway was a blond-haired boy. He spoke in an lilting English accent and looked about their age. "I've just moved to this town," he said, "and I wanted to sign up for dance class, but there doesn't seem to be anyone in the office."

Gwen sucked in her stomach. Zan bent her knees. McGee fluffed up her curly hair. Mary Bubnik let out a high-pitched giggle. None of them said a word.

Rocky, who had learned her lesson, smiled warmly. "You've come to the right place. Miss Delacorte is the receptionist, and she'll sign you up right away. Here, I'll introduce you."

The boy answered her with a dazzling smile. As Rocky took his arm and led him into the party, she turned back to her friends and whispered, "The vow starts tomorrow, OK?"

WIN A BAD NEWS BALLET SWEATSHIRT!

Enter the

Bad News Ballet

C O N T E S T !

Rocky, Zan, Mary Bubnik, Gwen, and McGee may not like to dance…but they sure can make you laugh! To them, ballet is *bad news*!

100 Winners!

But here's *great news* for you! You can win your very own Bad News Ballet sweatshirt. It's easy to enter the Bad News Ballet contest! Just complete the coupon below and return by August 31, 1989.

This fabulous big, oversized sweatshirt is pink with the Bad News Ballet logo on front! One size fits all! Wear it to your next dance rehearsal—or just for fun!

Rules: Entries must be postmarked by August 31, 1989. Contestants must be between the ages of 7 and 12. The winner will be picked at random from all eligible entries received. No purchase necessary. Valid only in the U.S.A. Employees of Scholastic Inc., affiliates, subsidiaries, and their families not eligible. Void where prohibited. The winner will be notified by mail.

Fill in your name, age, and address below or write the information on a 3″ × 5″ piece of paper and mail to:
THE BAD NEWS BALLET CONTEST, Scholastic Inc., Dept BNB, 730 Broadway, New York, NY 10003.

- -

The Bad News Ballet Sweatshirt Contest

Where did you get this book?

☐ Bookstore   ☐ Drug Store   ☐ Supermarket
☐ Discount Store   ☐ Book Club   ☐ Book Fair
☐ Other _____
                        specify

Name _____

Birthday _____ Age _____

Street _____

City, State, Zip _____

BNB108

America's Favorite Series

THE BABY-SITTERS CLUB®

by Ann M. Martin

Collect Them All!

The six girls at Stoneybrook Middle School get into all kinds of adventures...with school, boys, and, of course, baby-sitting!

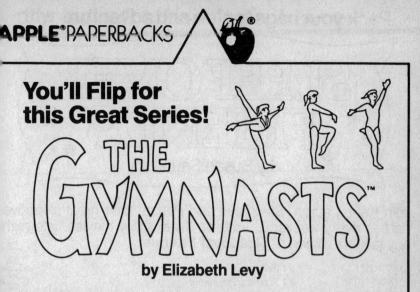

Pack your bags for fun and adventure with

SLEEPOVER FRIENDS™
by Susan Saunders

Join Kate, Lauren, Stephanie and Patti at their great sleepove
parties every weekend. Truth or Dare, scary movies, late-nigh
boy talk—it's all part of **Sleepover Friends!**